HACKER CLASS

A STORY OF
STEM INSPIRATION

SCOTT A. MILLER, P.E.

http://hackerclassbook.com

hackerclassbook@gmail.com

MW00880639

Written by Scott A. Miller.

Cover Design by Veronica Scott.

All rights reserved.   Except turning right on red.
That's not reserved.

This is a work of fiction.

ISBN 978-1-7378171-0-9 (paperback)
ISBN 978-1-7378171-1-6 (hardcover)

v2022.02.13

"When you want to know how things really work, study them when they're coming apart."

- William Gibson

This book is dedicated to the wonderful people who helped make it a reality:

Erika, English, Zac, Adelyn, Lincoln, Priscilla, David M., Michelle, Brian M., Kevin, Lynne, Brian S., Courtney, Sarah, Ayden, Darla, Veronica, David E., David T., David H., and Tom

And to these wonderful authors:

P.J. Hoover
PROBLEM SOLVERS: 15 Innovative Women Engineers and Coders
Tut: The Story of My Immortal Life

Dustin Brady
Trapped in a Video Game

CHAPTER 1

Alyssa didn't know what to expect. Rockets? Astronaut food? She had heard about weird astronaut ice cream.

She heard the pilot call out over the speaker: "Hello there folks, we are beginning our final descent into the Los Angeles International Airport. Please get those seat belts buckled and tray tables up."

Alyssa raised her tray table and opened the shade next to her. She enjoyed getting the window seat. She looked out the window as the plane tilted toward the ground. She saw the city. So many roads. It seemed to be a maze from so high above. So many places for the people and cars to go.

This was her first time to visit her Uncle Mikey in California. Uncle Mikey was an engineer for NASA. He had moved out to California a while ago, and this was her family's first time to visit him there, but Alyssa DEFI-NITELY remembered him. Since she was Uncle Mikey's first niece, he always had made it a point to spend time with her whenever he visited Texas.

She didn't know exactly what he worked on, but she thought NASA was awesome.

Uncle Mikey tried to be the "fun uncle". He did science experiments with her every time he came to visit. Sometimes messy science experiments, like the one time they made elephant toothpaste and it stained the driveway (which her parents were NOT happy about!). He would take her down to the corner store and get a Coke, just because. She had especially enjoyed the LEGO sets he brought her every time he came. She liked her uncle.

Before they left, Alyssa's mom told her Uncle Mikey wanted to take her to visit NASA.

She was super excited about this, but even though they had hung out before, she was intimidated. She felt like he knew SO much more than her.

Her mind snapped back to her surroundings as she felt the wheels of the airplane touch the ground. She heard her little brother squeal with excitement. She saw the metal sheets on the wings snap up to slow the airplane down. She had read they were called speed brakes, or something like that. She held onto the arms on the side of her seat as she experienced the slightly excited and slightly panicked feeling of a plane quickly slowing down.

She tapped her little brother and pointed out the window. "See, Lincoln? The metal pieces on top of the wing? Those are what slow us down. They're called speed brakes."

Lincoln bumped up and down, shouting "Let's do it again! Again! Again!". Her dad patted Lincoln on the head.

The plane came to a stop and she overheard the pilot again on the speaker: "Welcome to Los Angeles International Airport. We hope you have a safe and enjoyable visit here in the Golden State. Please wait until the seat-belt light goes off before you move about the cabin."

Alyssa gathered her bag from under the seat and took her phone out to turn it off of airplane mode. She wondered what airplane mode even did.

She kept staring out the window as she waited to get out of her seat. She finally heard the bell and saw the seatbelt light turn off. She was hunched over with her backpack on. There wasn't a lot of room to stand up in these airplanes. She followed her mom out of the airplane when it was their turn. It felt good to be able to stretch her legs.

The airport was busy. She walked with her family past all the other gates and airplanes. She thought about how amazing it was that people didn't bump into each other all the time. People on their phones. People pulling luggage. Weaving in and out.

Alyssa tapped her mom on the arm: "So Uncle Mikey is supposed to meet us here?"

Her mom replied: "Yep. He said he'll be waiting for us. He texted me. Once we get past these gates and go down the escalator, he should be there."

Alyssa reached the escalator and put her hand on the side as it took her down. She thought about how the es-calator's only job was to keep turning. All the time. She wondered how many times the escalator went around in a day.

When she got to the bottom, she looked around for her Uncle Mikey. She finally saw him. He was wearing a shirt with the NASA logo on it. And surfer shorts. It was the logo everyone recognized: the blue circle and the red stripe and the big NASA letters. She had heard it was called "the meatball".

"Uncle Mikey!" She and her brother ran towards her uncle. He leaned down and gave Alyssa a hug, and looked directly at her: "How's my favorite niece doing? Good to see you!"

Alyssa smiled.

They walked towards the baggage area as Alyssa's mom and her uncle chatted about the trip. As Alyssa walked behind them, she saw her uncle look over his shoulder and ask: "So I told your mom I could take you to my work to see what I do there. Interested?"

She wanted to shout "YES!!!", but she settled for a big smile and a "Sure!".

As they waited for the bags, she heard her uncle talk to her mom: "Since it's the weekend, I thought it would be better to visit today. I can show Alyssa around a little easier on a Saturday. Could we drive to my place, drop off your bags, and Alyssa and I could go to visit where I work?"

Alyssa's mom replied with a tired look and said: "Sounds wonderful. I'd like to take a rest. And from the looks of it, Lincoln could use one too. We were up quite early this morning!"

Uncle Mikey looked at Alyssa and said: "It's settled. The NASA visit will be today after we drop off your mom and brother."

Alyssa smiled and said: "Great!"

On the car ride to Uncle Mikey's house, she was shocked by the number of lanes on the highways. In her Texas hometown of Houston, she had seen six lanes on a highway, but this seemed even crazier. She counted TEN lanes on the highway they were on. She overheard her uncle say driving on "the four-o-five" was about as much fun as going to the dentist.

When they arrived at Uncle Mikey's house, they unloaded their bags and got a quick snack. As he finished his drink, Uncle Mikey asked: "Well, ready?"

Alyssa picked up her Coke: "Sure, but I need to finish my drink first. Don't want to spill it in your car."

Her uncle picked up the keys and said "The carpet in a car can't stay clean forever. Bring it with you. No problem. It'll be fine."

Alyssa knew her mom would never allow an open Coke in the car. Her mom shook her head, laughed, and said "Alright, alright, it's your car. Y'all have fun."

Uncle Mikey and Alyssa started walking toward the door. He yelled back to Alyssa's mom: "Y'all buckaroos have fun too!" Her Uncle Mikey liked to give Alyssa's mom a hard time about the Texan words like "y'all" she used.

As they drove, Uncle Mikey asked Alyssa: "So, what's new in your world?   You're going into sixth grade this year?"

"Yep.   Sixth grade. It's a new school. But it's close to the elementary school I was in last year."

He asked her: "Looking forward to it?"

"I think so. I know a lot of kids going there. Almost all of my class from last year."

Then she remembered what she had wanted to tell Uncle Mikey.

"Oh yeah! I'signed up for a STEM class! There's this teacher called Ms. Powers. She came to talk to us last year about signing up for it as an elective. It looks pretty neat. I'm excited."

"Cool! Sounds like you are looking forward to it."

"Yeah, I think it's going to be fun. I heard we get to learn programming and robots.   And Ms. Powers seems like a good teacher. Maybe I'll even learn how to be a hacker."

Uncle Mikey responded: "A hacker, huh? Cool. What kind of hacking do you think you'll do?"

She replied: "Well I know kids talk about hacking video

games and stuff. And I've seen in the news talk about hackers breaking into computer systems. I don't want to be a bad person breaking into systems or anything. But it would be cool to be able to understand all that."

Her uncle responded: "Did you know I'm a hacker too?"

She turned toward him and raised an eyebrow. "You're a hacker? Do you even play video games?"

He laughed. "Ummm…probably more than I should. But I'm probably not talking about the hacking you're thinking of."

"What do you mean?", Alyssa asked.

As they went past the security guard at the entrance, he explained: "Well, I'm talking about hacking in a different way. I'm talking about creating. I don't break into servers or video games or anything. That's hacking, sure. But I build parts for spacecraft. And to me, that's kind of like hacking."

Alyssa replied: "I've always wondered exactly what you do at NASA. So do we get to see rockets today?"

"Kind of", said Uncle Mikey. They turned into the parking lot in front of a large building.

She followed Uncle Mikey to the doors at the building in front of there and he scanned his badge. She heard the door beep and saw a light turn green. He opened the door for Alyssa.

As they walked down the hallway, her uncle pointed through a large glass window and said: "See that? The thing with six wheels and a big robot arm? Kinda looks like a weird monster truck? That's the Mars rover I'm working on. Cool, right?'"

She was pretty sure this was the COOLEST thing she had ever seen.

"This place is called the 'clean room'. Keeps the equipment going into space from getting dirty. Even a small amount of dust can mess up important parts. We are not done testing, but we are close to the grand finale! It launches in November, right before Thanksgiving."

Uncle Mikey opened a door at the end of a hallway. They went through and he raised his hands like a referee at a football game. "Well, this is it!"

Alyssa saw LOTS of computers. There were tables everywhere with monitors, electronics, and all kinds of parts and pieces she didn't recognize.

"This is what? This is where you work?"

He led her past the tables. "Yep. This is the lab. This is where the fun happens."

She saw small models of the rover, papers with drawings EVERYWHERE, tools, wires, and electronics. She even saw a roll of aluminum foil, and wondered what on earth it could be for. She saw rows and rows of computers, each with HUGE monitors connected to them. She wondered if they ever played games on the huge monitors. She would.

They arrived at a table where she saw what she figured was Uncle Mikey's computer. She saw a few pictures on his desk of her uncle and her grandparents. She saw a family picture with her in it.

Uncle Mikey pointed at a table with a variety of metal pieces and circuit boards. "This table is where I break things!"

Alyssa was confused. "Break things?"

He smiled. "Well, not like tearing them apart when I'm angry or anything. More like making things better. This is what I call hacking."

She looked at the electronics boards on the table. "I'm still confused. That's not what I've seen on the internet about hacking. I thought it was all about computers. You know, with the black boxes all over the screen and all the green text."

Her uncle picked up a circuit board. "Sure. That's hacking. But this is too."

He gave the board to Alyssa. She asked: "Can I touch this? Are you sure?"

Uncle Mikey said: "Yep. This is actually a broken one. We accidentally messed it up a year or two ago. One of the parts on the board was backwards, and when we tried to fix it, we damaged it. See the big black mark? It's one of the first prototypes. Prototypes are your first few tries."

Alyssa flipped the board over in her hands. She asked: "So how does this thing work?"

Uncle Mikey answered: "I like to think of these types of boards as a humongous maze. Look at the gold paths on the green board. And all the tiny chips on it. And resistors. And capacitors. That's the maze. There are millions of ways electricity can move around on it. And like every maze, there are a LOT of wrong ways to go through the maze, but there are right ways too."

He continued: "My team's job is to figure out how to get the electricity on this board to move through the maze, do the right actions at the right time, and eventually, control the robot arm on the rover this board is attached to. This arm is going to pick up soil samples on Mars for scientists to analyze."

"Sooo cool!", exclaimed Alyssa.

"Yep, I've been super lucky. This has been a neat project to work on."

"So this is hacking to you?" asked Alyssa.

Uncle Mikey replied: "Well, that's what I think. You'll have to decide for yourself. Hacking can mean something different to you than it means to me, or anyone else."

Alyssa gave him the board back. "It's awesome to hold a piece of a Mars Rover, even if it isn't quite the real thing."

Uncle Mikey pointed at another area of the lab. "Let's go look at some of the other parts for different projects."

He walked past the other tables and showed her power supplies, prototypes of a camera for the rover, and even some of the first prototypes for the rover wheels. She saw a pit that looked like a HUGE sandbox. She guessed it was for testing the wheels.

They spent about an hour looking around the lab. As they walked through another hallway with glass windows, he pointed out an area with lots of computers called an "operations center". Uncle Mikey explained to her that for missions already in operation, spacecraft were mostly taking care of themselves, but engineers in the operations center would routinely look at the incoming data and command the spacecraft.

They walked towards the exit of the building and hung up their blue lab coats. Uncle Mikey said they were for electrostatic discharge, or something like that. Whatever they were for, it was cool to have a coat on like a real scientist. Like the ones she saw in textbooks with the glasses and a chemistry beaker.

Uncle Mikey pointed down a hallway and squinted. "Let's take this hallway down to the parking lot. I don't usually go this way, but I think it's shorter."

When they reached the end of the hallway, Uncle Mikey pushed the door. It wouldn't budge. He looked for a place to scan his card. There was none. He started wondering out loud if the door was broken.

Alyssa noticed a sign by the door. She spoke up: "Umm…Uncle Mikey? The door says you have to pull. Not push."

Uncle Mikey shook his head and laughingly said, "Of course!" He pulled the door open.

Alyssa smiled too. Maybe Uncle Mikey wasn't as close to perfect as she thought.

They walked out of the building towards Uncle Mikey's car.

Alyssa asked: "So what type of engineer are you? I've read there are a lot of types."

Uncle Mikey replied: "Many years ago, I got a degree in mechanical engineering, but what I learned in school is only part of what I use in my job today. I've had to learn lots of different skills as I've gotten older. There's no way I could do my job if I didn't keep learning. I've learned how to make circuit boards. Software. How to solder. I even had to learn how to speak a little bit of German for one project! Kind of like collecting objects in different worlds in a video game: I go where I need to pick up pieces of knowledge, then move on."

Alyssa said: "Cool. Thanks for bringing me here Uncle Mikey. I hope my class teaches me all about the types of things you do. I wish I could tell you about what I learn in class."

Uncle Mikey replied: "Well, maybe we could make it happen. Video chat is easy these days. How about you and me can talk about class every now and then? You can tell me what you are learning about and how your class is going, and I'll tell you what I'm learning and how my projects at NASA are going."

Alyssa was a bit surprised. "REALLY? That would be so amazing!"

Uncle Mikey said: "Hey Siri, FaceTime Alyssa."

Alyssa's phone rang. She smiled as Uncle Mikey said: "We can FaceTime, and you've gotta text me too. Totes cool?"

Alyssa laughed at her Uncle Mikey trying to use a word like "totes". She smiled and said: "Yeah, totes cool."

On the ride home, Alyssa thought about what she would tell her uncle about. She was a little intimidated thinking about what she would say. Would he even think it's interesting? Would he think she didn't know what she was talking about?

When they arrived at Uncle Mikey's house, Alyssa's mom greeted them as they came through the door: "Howdy! Y'all have a good trip to your Uncle's work?"

Alyssa walked into the kitchen. "It was so cool! Uncle Mikey wouldn't let me take the robot arm home, but I learned a lot of stuff!"

Uncle Mikey laughed. "I'm not sure NASA has an extra

robot arm for you! But I'll send you another picture of it on the rover before launch."

Alyssa turned to her mom and said: "Mom, Uncle Mikey and I are going to video chat about my STEM class and what he's been doing!"

Alyssa's mom replied: "Sounds great to me. I'm glad you two will be staying in touch.   Hard for you guys to visit in person too much. California is pretty far from Texas!"

Alyssa's mom pointed at Uncle Mikey's shorts with surfboards on it: "The surfing waves aren't quite as big in Texas!   And we don't eat avocado toast too much, or whatever it is y'all like here."

Uncle Mikey picked up his phone and said: "Ha, ha, ha. I'll have avocado toast next week. How about pizza tonight?"

Alyssa and her mom nodded their heads.   Her dad gave a thumbs up. "Sounds good to me!", said Alyssa. Lincoln yelled "Yay! Pizza!"

Alyssa pulled up her phone to see what pizza places were around on a map.   Since it was her first time to Los Angeles, she was curious what the city looked like zoomed out. She kept pinching her fingers on the phone so she could see the whole city. It reminded her of how it looked when she had seen it from the airplane. It looked like a maze. She liked mazes.

CHAPTER 2

The first day of sixth grade STEM class was not exactly what Alyssa thought it would be.

It wasn't that she was at a different school. Her new middle school was about what she had expected. She knew where most places were, and had only messed up once going down the wrong hallway to find her classes on her first day. STEM was one of her last classes of the day.

Class started out normal enough. Ms. Powers took attendance, passed out some books, and explained the rules of the class. Like all the other classes so far.

Alyssa looked around for her friend Adelyn.

The week earlier, her best friend Adelyn told Alyssa she signed up for the class too. Adelyn and Alyssa had been best friends since first grade.

But Alyssa didn't see Adelyn. There was only one STEM class for sixth graders, so Alyssa figured it was probably a first day schedule mixup or something. She'd see her after school.

Ms. Powers finished up her introduction to the class: when homework would be given, what materials they would need, how assignments would be graded, how students could check their grades, yada yada yada. They did a quick get-to-know-you activity, but Ms. Powers was apparently incredibly excited and wanted to jump right into the first lesson: a kit to teach them about electricity.

Ms. Powers told the class two people would pair up for each kit, and they would be partners for the semester. Alyssa became concerned. Extremely concerned. Where was Adelyn? She thought about asking Ms. Powers if she could wait until the next day for Adelyn to show, but she decided against it.

Ms. Powers asked the students to pair themselves into a group. Most students found someone they already knew or chose the person at the desk next to them. Ms. Powers asked anyone who didn't have a partner to raise their hand. There were only two hands raised. Alyssa and a boy she didn't know. Ms. Powers said "Perfect! Alyssa, you and Ethan will be in a group."

Wait WHAT? A boy she didn't even know, for the rest of the semester? Wonderful, just wonderful.

Ethan moved desks next to Alyssa: "Hey."

Alyssa was not excited about the situation, but she put on a fake smile and begrudgingly said: "Hi. I'm Alyssa."

"Is this your first STEM class?" asked Ethan.

Alyssa replied: "Yeah…I've never done anything like this before. But I'm excited about it. I want to learn."

Ethan responded: "I've been going to STEM summer camps for a few years now."

Alyssa replied: "Cool."

Neither of them was quite sure what else to say, so they waited in silence for Ms. Powers to talk. It was an awkward few seconds.

Ms. Powers came around to each pair of students to pass out the kit. As she walked, she said: "The kit we will work on today will help you learn about electricity. When you open the kit, you'll find a battery, a light, a switch, some wires, and a few other pieces we will use after the first experiment. Your task is to connect the pieces in the first experiment so the switch turns on the light."

After she passed out the kits, she raised her hands and said: "To the magic school bus!".

"Just kidding!", said Ms. Powers. "Go ahead and open your kits and get to work! The instructions are inside."

Alyssa was excited. Her first STEM kit! Ethan and Alyssa pulled the materials out of the bags, spread out the pieces, and started to read the instructions for the first experiment. Ethan put out the instructions so Alyssa could see them too.

After reading them, Ethan said "Ok. So for the first part, we connect the battery to the wires, then we connect the wires to the light."

She watched Ethan put it together. She was a little annoyed he didn't seem to want to let her do anything, but she was also glad he seemed to know what he was doing.

She thought she could learn quickly. It seemed simple enough. After it was connected, he flipped the switch a few times and saw the light go on and off.

Ethan said: "Watch this".

Ethan took a few other parts out of the kit Ms. Powers hadn't told them about yet and started hooking them up. Alyssa watched with interest. What was he doing?

"Check this out. I hooked up some resistors in the circuit. Now if you turn this knob I hooked up, it changes how bright the light is."

Alyssa turned the knob. "Whoa, cool! It does change the brightness. How did you know how to do that?"

Ethan replied: "STEM camp. I remember this kit. Here, we'll take it apart so you know how to put it together."

Maybe Ethan wouldn't be a bad teammate after all. She decided she'd give him a chance.

Ms. Powers walked around and made sure everyone was able to get the light to turn on. She stopped by Alyssa's desk. She seemed pleased and said: "Excellent! I see you two have skipped ahead a bit! Very nice." She continued walking around. Alyssa was happy she hadn't gotten upset they had skipped ahead. Ms. Powers was a good teacher so far.

After everyone had gotten the light to turn on, Ms. Powers went to the whiteboard and described electricity as wanting to move through a maze. With this kit, a simple maze. Straight from one end of the battery, through the light, then back to the other end of the battery. Like cars driving on a one way street around a park. The cars were the electrons. The switch was the traffic cop. And when the cars were allowed to drive, the light turned on.

Alyssa remembered her Uncle Mikey talked about electricity running through a maze.

Ms. Powers continued on about electricity. She talked about adding the resistor, and how it turned some of the energy into heat. Like cars that took the off-ramp from the highway and didn't go back to the battery.

The class worked through the next experiment with the resistor. Ethan helped other groups putting it together. Alyssa looked through the instructions and the handout Ms. Powers had given about electricity.

The bell rang. Alyssa put the electricity kit back in the bag for Ms. Powers to pick up.

After school, Alyssa looked for Adelyn in the courtyard. All summer, they had talked about how they would walk home with each other. Alyssa saw her, and Adelyn waved.

Alyssa said "Hey! So, I didn't see you in STEM class today. Must have been a schedule mix-up or something. Did you get it fixed?"

Adelyn hunched her shoulders and replied: "Ummm.... not a schedule mixup. A few days ago, I decided to sign up for soccer instead of STEM. The classes are at the same time, and I had to choose one. My mom called the school and changed my schedule last Friday. I hope you're not mad."

Alyssa was confused. "What? I thought you and I were going to take the STEM class together? That's what we talked about last week! You didn't tell me? We even had math together today and you didn't tell me then!"

Adelyn replied: "I know, Alyssa, and I'm sorry. I didn't want to disappoint you. I couldn't decide. But I eventually signed up because I think I'll like it. I'm going to try out for soccer, basketball, volleyball, everything I can. My brother Zac is going to be on the soccer team next year at his high school. I've been to a lot of his games."

Alyssa didn't know what to think. She sighed. "I guess we still have math together."

She was mad and sad at the same time.

After walking in silence for a while, wanting to change the subject, Adelyn told Alyssa about a dog named Belle her family was fostering. Alyssa's parents didn't want pets, and Alyssa loved to go to Adelyn's house to play with the pets they had.

As the girls reached Adelyn's house, they could both hear Belle barking from the backyard. Adelyn opened the gate.

"Hi Belle!" Alyssa exclaimed.

The dog raced around them in a circle. "Whoa, settle down girl!" Adelyn shouted.

Adelyn made Belle sit, and walked her to the front of the house. She wiped some dog fur off of her.

"What do you think?"

Alyssa combed her fingers through Belle's fur and replied: "She's awesome. I hope your family decides to keep her."

Adelyn's mom opened the front door and called for Belle. She shouted: "Hi Alyssa! Adelyn, please come inside, we need to leave in an hour."

Adelyn picked up her backpack to go inside. As she ushered Belle through her front door, she said: "See you tomorrow, Alyssa. I'm sorry about not being in STEM class."

Alyssa waved bye.

She continued her walk home. Why didn't her BEST friend want to take the class with her? Did she not want to be best friends anymore? Was she scared of taking the class? Alyssa had been kind of annoyed when Ethan seemed to know everything, but she figured she was as smart as he was. Didn't Adelyn know she could be just as smart too?

Alyssa would be upset about her friend bailing on her for a while. But seeing the dog had made it a little better.

Alyssa walked into her house, and hung up her coat. "I'm home, mom!"

Alyssa's mom turned around as she was putting away some toys and replied: "Hey Alyssa! How was your first day?"

Alyssa replied: "It was good." Even though she wanted to vent, she was tired, and didn't feel like elaborating much. And she didn't want her mom quizzing her about her class disappointment.

Her mom replied: "Great. I want to hear more later. Oh, by the way, Uncle Mikey texted me. Something about you and him having a video chat?"

"Oh Yeah!" replied Alyssa. "I'm going to talk with Uncle Mikey about my STEM class!"

After dinner, Alyssa ran upstairs. She dialed Uncle Mikey on video chat. He answered on the first ring.

"Alyssa! So, first day! Did you build a spaceship in class?", asked Uncle Mikey.

Alyssa laughed: "No, not quite. We started learning about electricity."

"Hard to build a spaceship without electricity! Not a bad subject to start with." said Uncle Mikey.

Alyssa continued: "STEM class was pretty neat. I like the teacher. We did a fun project with a light today. But...

class wasn't exactly perfect."

"What do you mean?" asked Uncle Mikey.

She hesitated a bit. She didn't know if she wanted to tell Uncle Mikey about Adelyn. But she figured he probably wouldn't quiz her about it. It would be good to talk to someone.

Alyssa responded: "Well, my best friend Adelyn, who said she would sign up for the class, decided she'd rather do athletics this year. Not STEM. She told me last week she was going to! So she's not going to be my partner in the class. I'm pretty upset."

Uncle Mikey replied: "Sorry Alyssa. That's tough. So who did you end up in a group with?"

Alyssa answered "This boy I've never met before. His name is Ethan. He seems nice though. And he's been to a few STEM camps."

Uncle Mikey responded: "Well that's cool at least. It's always good to have someone to be able to learn from. I guess you can give him a chance."

Alyssa silently agreed. It was quiet for a few seconds.

Uncle Mikey continued: "I had something similar happen to me. My friend, Mark, and I started out working at NASA on the same project several years ago. We worked well together. He became one of my best friends. We went to lunch together almost every day. I thought we would work on many more projects together. But about a year ago, Mark decided he wanted to move to a place with colder weather. I was bummed."

He continued: "I don't see Mark much anymore. We told each other we would visit, but you know how it goes. For a while, I worked by myself on the project. But it was still fun. Eventually, other people got assigned to my project. They've been great. I have new lunch friends now."

Alyssa responded: "My friend Adelyn is looking forward to playing sports. Her older brother plays on the high school soccer team, and now I guess she wants to play soccer too."

Uncle Mikey replied: "Sometimes you are going to have interests none of your friends enjoy. And there's nothing wrong with that. You aren't ever going to be able to get away from yourself! You might as well enjoy hanging out with your own self!"

Alyssa replied: "I guess so. Adelyn and I do have another class and lunch break together. And we both still enjoy other activities together. Like dogs. So I guess we still do have a few things in common. Soccer will be her thing. I guess STEM can be my thing."

Alyssa wanted to change the topic. She asked: "So how is your project going?"

Uncle Mikey replied: "Well, today could have been better. We were doing some of our tests with the robot arm, and it was going great, until one of the small pieces on the end snapped off! The piece was dragging too hard on the surface we were scraping. It didn't completely break the robot arm, and it wouldn't be the end of the world if it broke on Mars, but it wasn't good. We had to take it all apart, order a replacement piece, and get ready to try it again. The new part doesn't come in until Wednesday."

Alyssa asked: "So what do you do until then?"

Uncle Mikey replied: "Well, that's the fun part. It was disappointing it broke, but that's why we tested. You can't expect new tests to always work on the first try. We have to figure out what went wrong and how to fix it. We have to find the root cause."

Alyssa asked "What's the root cause?"

Uncle Mikey replied: "The root cause is the first domino to fall. It's the first thing to go wrong. It's like when you are pulling weeds out of a garden. If you pull out a weed by the root, it won't come back. But if you don't get the root, you'll see the weed again soon enough. We could fix our problem by changing how deep the dirt is, but that wouldn't be fixing the root cause. You don't exactly have control over how deep the dirt is on Mars! The root cause is probably somewhere in our software or hardware. Don't know yet. But we'll figure it out."

Alyssa replied: "I think I get it. So the root cause is what you have to fix so it definitely won't break again."

Uncle Mikey replied: "Exactly."

CHAPTER 3

Alyssa saw Ethan wave to her in the hall in the passing period before STEM class.

She figured she was stuck with him for a while, so she might as well get to know him. She waved back.

Ethan looked excited.

"Hey, did you hear? We are going to a Maker Faire!"

"A Maker Faire?" asked Alyssa.

Ethan responded: "It's a bunch of booths with awesome science exhibits. I think it's going to be downtown. I went to one last summer at the end of camp."

They walked through the classroom door. Alyssa put her bag down.

She asked: "Like a science fair? What kind of exhibits are we going to see?"

Ethan responded: "Well, not exactly like a science fair. Kind of like one, but most of the exhibits have activities you can play with and look at. Not just posters. I've only been to one, but I'm guessing we will see robots, games, 3D printers, experiments, things like that. Maybe one of the science YouTubers I like to watch will be there!"

Alyssa laughed: "I'd be surprised if any YouTubers were there. But it sounds sweet."

She cringed when she used the word "sweet". She had heard her dad say it.

Ms. Powers had a "STEM Squad" shirt and the room was decorated with posters of famous scientists and every type of engineering you could think of. She saw a poster that said "Science is like magic but real!"

The bell rang. Ms. Powers started the class. "Welcome my students! I have SUPER exciting news!"

She continued: "In two weekends, there will be a field trip to a Maker Faire in this wonderful city of Houston we call home! A Maker Faire is a gathering of people who love to create. We'll see all kinds of neat ways people use engineering, science, and creativity. There will be no boring poster presentations at this event. It will be all hands-on!"

She added: "And if that wasn't cool enough for you, I've got other good news! The companies sponsoring the Maker Faire have also donated money to our class to buy kits for your upcoming projects! You'll get to choose from several nice kits. After the Maker Faire, I'll give you flyers about the options you have to choose from."

This class was moving fast. Ms. Powers passed out the permission slips to be signed by the parents for attending the Maker Faire.

As Ms. Powers walked back to the front, she spoke: "So I'm about to make you all feel like a first grader again. There may be a few of you who remember the Magic School Bus. The Magic School Bus may seem like it's for children. It is! But there's a reason it works with elementary students. It's simple. And it's fun. Just because you are older, don't think you can't learn something from good ol' Ms. Frizzle."

As the video went through the opening credits, she continued: "Ms. Frizzle explains topics in a fun and simple way. This is extremely important! She focuses on the basics, imagines being small, and uses lots of analogies."

Ms. Powers dimmed the lights as the class turned their attention to the screen.

It had been several years since Alyssa had read a Magic School Bus book or watched the show. Alyssa thought maybe her little brother Lincoln still had some of the books. She secretly enjoyed having ideas explained to her by a crazy teacher and a magical bus usually shown to first graders. She looked around the class. Maybe others felt the same way. She saw a few of them trying to hold back a smile.

The next few days of class went by quickly. The class worked through assignments and learned from Ms. Powers as she continued teaching about electricity.

Two weeks went by quickly. Finally, the Saturday of the field trip had arrived, and the bus waited at the middle school to take them to the Maker Faire. Alyssa arrived at the pick-up area in plenty of time and was waiting in line to board, but she didn't see Ethan. She didn't know anyone else in the class, and figured she could at least talk to him on the bus ride.

Ms. Powers looked up from her clipboard: "OK class! Time to board the bus!"

Alyssa felt her phone vibrate, and saw a text from Ethan. They had traded numbers the day before. "Sorry. Running late, will meet u there."

Alyssa was relieved, but kind of annoyed. Now she didn't have anyone to sit with on the bus.

She didn't want to seem irritated in the text back to Ethan, so she responded "k."

As Alyssa boarded the bus and walked down the aisle, she looked for open seats. There weren't many. She saw one near the back. She decided to sit next to a girl had seen in class, but hadn't talked to before.

"Hi. I'm Alyssa. What's your name?"

"Hi." The girl said, " I'm Madison."

Alyssa asked: "Excited about the Maker Faire?"

Madison turned her eyes toward the window: "I guess so. Maybe."

Alyssa asked: "Just maybe?"

Madison responded: "'Yeah, maybe. I signed up for a STEM class this year because I didn't know what else to pick and my parents thought I should. I guess it's been OK. Ms. Powers is cool. Maybe the Maker Faire will be fun."

Alyssa replied: "I heard there are snacks there!"

Madison half-smiled: "Well that's good at least."

Alyssa learned Madison sort of wanted to take the class because her dad worked with computers, but she didn't know if she would enjoy it.

The bus arrived at the Maker Faire. The event was at a HUGE arena.

The class got off the bus and they followed Ms. Powers towards the entrance. Madison and Alyssa walked together. As they got close to the entrance of the stadium, Alyssa saw Ethan being dropped off by his parents.

Alyssa yelled "Ethan! Over here!" Ethan ran over and joined in with the group.

The class stopped walking, and Alyssa saw Ms. Powers talking with the event organizers. Her teacher passed around the lanyards to be worn with a bright green sticker so she knew who was in her class.

"Class, you will be visiting the exhibits in groups no bigger than four. Please join together and raise your hands when you have a group."

Madison had told Alyssa her partner, Danny, wasn't able to come to the Maker Faire.

Alysa looked at Madison. Ethan looked at Alyssa. They formed a group of three.

Ms. Powers counted up the groups and wrote down everyone's names and released them to visit the exhibits.

It didn't take long before the group was visiting their first booth. Right at the entrance, there was a huge display of video games. Humongous monitors, gaming consoles, flight simulators, and building games. It looked more like an arcade than a STEM exhibit.

One of the booth's workers walked up to the group of three and asked "Are you guys into video games?"

Ethan replied: "Yes!"

Alyssa and Madison nodded their heads.

The booth worker told them: "I'm Matt. This exhibit is to show you what it's like to be a video game designer. And of course, we have video games to play too. Which I'm sure none of you are interested in playing today."

They knew he was joking. Matt smiled and continued: "I'm sure I'm wrong about that. You'll get your turn, absolutely. But first let me show you the types of things I work on."

He led them to a computer with a modeling program open. It looked like he was working on a game like

Minecraft, but not quite the same. It had more detail than Minecraft. It wasn't as "blocky". He started moving around objects and zooming in and out.

Matt explained: "This is what I work on. I help create new levels for video games where you build maps. I work with the artists and designers who tell me what they'd like to see. I create levels."

He continued: "When I was in high school, I enjoyed math, and I liked to doodle and draw. I ended up going to college and earning a math degree, and I ended up here."

Alyssa asked: "So if you create the levels do you know how kids can hack into them?"

Matt replied: "Well, if you mean hacking like 'breaking into the game', no not so much. I create. To me, creating is hacking".

She could see Uncle Mikey in her head saying: "See? Hacking can also be creating. Told ya so." She shook her head and grinned.

Madison asked Matt: "So what are you working on next?"

Matt replied: "Funny you should ask that. I want you guys to learn about what I'm doing now, but, it just so turns out I'm about to change jobs. I've enjoyed working on video games for several years now, but I just told my boss last week I've accepted a job offer in another city to work at a company that makes laptops."

Alyssa asked: "You're leaving a company where you make video games to a company making laptops?"

She couldn't believe it. Everyone wanted to make video games.

Matt replied: "I've been doing this for a while, and I've decided for me, it's the right thing to do. This next job will be closer to my family, and I think I'll enjoy it. I'm going to use a lot of the skills I learned at this job at my next one. I'm going to be designing the cases for laptops. Those need good designers too. It may not sound as cool as creating video games, but I think it will be fun to me."

One of the other booth workers called over for Matt to join him. Matt pointed out the video at the exit of the booth: "Looks like one of my co-workers needs me. The line for the video games has died down a bit. Feel free to play a few levels. Enjoy!"

The group played the games while Alyssa thought about how weird it was for Matt to want to stop being a videogame designer. It didn't make any sense. Didn't he like doing something so awesome?

When they finished playing, the group looked out at the maze of what else to visit.

Alyssa said: "Hey! Check it out! Cookies!"

They walked to the exhibit and picked up some cookies. Behind the table at the exhibit was a baker. With a white hat and apron. He looked like a baker out of a children's book.

A group had started to form around the booth, and they heard the baker talking: "And I'm sure the cookies are a big reason you're here!".

He bit into a cookie and closed his eyes: "Mmmm. Chocolate chip."

He wiped his face with a napkin and continued: "Now I know what you're thinking. I have no business presenting at a STEM exhibit. And you'd be right, if you didn't know what STEM was!"

He motioned to a table in front of him with baking equipment.

He continued: "When most people think of STEM, they imagine robots, computers and electronics. But there are a lot of things all of us use and enjoy every day that don't require pressing buttons on a keyboard."

"I'm immensely glad there are people who create robots, but the electronics in a robot don't taste too good. My job is to create. I create yummy treats."

"The treats I create don't come from me getting ingredients out of a pantry. I have tools I use. And I'm here at this exhibit day because I created several tools to help me bake. Take, for instance, this mixer."

He picked up a mixer from the table of baking equipment.

"I created a special tool that mixes the batter to just the right consistency. I worked with a team to modify the mixer so it stops when the batter gets to the right thickness. The right thickness for me means more enjoyable cookies for you! I've also created several other inventions. Some of them are probably not great ideas, but some of them have turned out especially well. I've set them out on the table here. Take a look! And grab a cookie!"

Alyssa knew she didn't want to be a baker, but she knew she liked cookies.

The group of three walked around to several more exhibits. They explored until it was time to meet the class to go back to the bus. They saw 3D printing stations, virtual reality booths, robot pinball machines, and drone racing.

Ms. Powers saw the group of three as they were walking back. She joined them and asked: "Well, my wonderful students, what did you see today?"

Ethan said: "All all kinds of things. We saw drone racing! But the video game designer was probably my favorite. And we even saw someone who did an experiment to find out if a banana is actually slippery. That was kind of cool."

Madison didn't seem to want to say much, but she smiled when Ethan told Ms. Powers about drone racing.

Ms. Powers replied: "Well that's quite a creative experiment. I've always wondered how slippery they actually are. Are you interested in any of the areas you saw today?"

Alyssa responded: "The video game designer was cool, but I'd probably never be able to be one."

Ms. Powers asked: "And why is that?"

Alyssa told Ms. Powers: "I'm not creative. I've never been someone who imagines a lot."

Ms. Powers replied: "Indeed. If you haven't done it much, you probably wouldn't be especially good at it."

What? Weren't teachers supposed to be encouraging? Why would Ms. Powers say something like that?

Ms. Powers explained: "If I said I wasn't any good at basketball, but I didn't practice, would you be surprised? Probably not, right? Artists always have erasers for when they make mistakes."

Alyssa had heard adults tell her OVER and OVER if she wanted to be creative or get good at something, she could work on it. But she wasn't sure if she believed them.

As the students boarded the bus, Ms. Powers passed out flyers. As she passed them out, she explained: "As promised, these flyers show the kits you can choose from for your project. The project you pick will be presented at the end of the semester at our own school's Maker Faire!"

This time, Ethan and Alyssa sat together on the bus. Madison was across from them. Ethan and Alyssa looked at the flyer. There were lots of options. Robots. Drones. Mini Solar-Cars. She saw one that caught her attention: The Crane Kit.

Alyssa shouted: "Look at that one! The Crane Kit! It looks awesome!"

The kit looked like a super complicated LEGO set. But it had metal parts too. It had wheels. It reminded her of the Mars Rover her uncle was working on. It looked like it could be steered around. It had a hook that went up and down. And maybe side to side? It seemed like it was pretty close to a real crane. There were manual controls buttons to steer it around and raise and lower the hook, AND it even showed an app you could use on a phone.

Ethan looked at the Crane Kit on his flyer. "That does look cool. It looks like it can actually move too. Like a toy monster truck, but with a crane on it!"

Alyssa replied: "It's no NASA robot arm, but I like it."

Ethan asked: "So, this one? The Crane Kit?"

Alyssa excitedly said, "Absolutely! I'll let Ms. Powers know as SOON as we get off the bus."

CHAPTER 4

In STEM class, Ms. Powers told the students their kits would show in about two weeks.

After school, Alyssa was hoping to meet Adelyn for their Friday walk home. Alyssa had been hoping they would see each other outside class more than once a week, but Adelyn had soccer practice after school most days, and they didn't have the same lunch period. It was Friday, so Alyssa waited in their normal spot to meet, but Alyssa wasn't anywhere to be seen. Alyssa started her lonely walk home. As soon as she began walking, she heard a voice behind her.

"Alyssa!"

Alyssa turned around and smiled. Adelyn ran ahead to catch up.

Alyssa saw Adelyn was dressed in an athletics shirt. As Adelyn slowed down from running, Alyssa asked: "Nice athletics shirt. How's sports going?"

Adelyn replied: "The coaches are good, and I've gotten to spend a lot of time outside. I'm trying out for a soccer position soon. I hope I get the position I want."

Alyssa asked: "So, you're glad you signed up for it? Instead of STEM class?"

Adelyn replied: "Yes! But I'm glad I'm getting the chance to play sports."

Alyssa continued: "Cool. How about your other classes? Do you like them?"

Adelyn answered: "Most of them. I like language arts and science. Social studies is OK. We keep having substitute teachers, and they aren't as good, but our regular teacher is supposed to be back next week."

Alyssa filled her in on her own classes. "Yeah, the same thing happened to me in science in the first week of school. The sub was kinda strange."

Alyssa continued: "But the STEM class has been fun. I made a new friend, Ethan, and he seems like he knows what he's doing. We went to a Maker Faire, where they have exhibits of inventors, creators, and experiments. We talked to a video game designer. And we saw a baker who made cookies and told us about how he used science with his equipment!"

Adelyn laughed: "A baker? Weird. But speaking of food, why don't we head to my house for a bit, have a snack and catch up? I can show you what I learned at soccer practice."

Alyssa was disappointed Adelyn didn't seem interested in her class, but said: "Sure. I'm in."

Alyssa and Adelyn finished the walk to Alyssa's house, set down their bags, and headed to the kitchen. Alyssa's older brother Zac was looking at phone cases on the counter.

Adelyn offered Alyssa some chips and turned to her brother: "What's with the phone cases?"

Her brother replied: "Oh, I'm looking at different designs. I'm making phone cases so I can sell them."

Alyssa asked: "Making phone cases? You can do that?"

Zac answered: "Yeah, I've been reading about it. When I dropped my phone and it almost cracked, I started looking around on the Internet for phone cases. But instead of buying one, I saw a few how-to articles online, and I'm going to try making them."

Alyssa was curious: "How do you make them?"

Zac replied: "Well, I'm not completely sure of everything yet, but, I'm going to do it with hot glue, parchment paper, tape, and a few painting materials. I'm still learning what I need, and I have some experiments to do."

Alyssa asked: "So, are you going to make a lot of money when you sell them?"

Zac laughed and replied: "Maybe. I'm going to sell them for twenty dollars per case. My friends might buy one, but they're not interested in helping me make them. But I'm good with that. Just a hobby to have. And I might make a few bucks."

Alyssa and Adelyn had a few more snacks, practiced soccer, played some video games, and did their homework together. When it was time for dinner, Alyssa went home.

When she got home, since it had been a few weeks since they last talked, Alyssa decided to call Uncle Mikey. Adelyn hadn't been too interested in what she had to say about STEM class, and she wanted someone to tell about it.

Alyssa called Uncle Mikey. When he answered, it took him a bit to get the phone pointed toward him. He looked like he was working on something outside his house.

He answered: "Hey! One second. I'm working on the house. Let me find a seat."

Alyssa saw him walk around and take a seat.

He sat, wiped his forehead and said: "There we go. Now I'm sitting. So, are y'all working on a Moon Lander in class?"

Alyssa laughed and replied: "I'm not sure what school you think I go to! Not quite yet!"

Uncle Mikey laughed and asked: "Moon landers are hard. So, in more real news, how is class? Did anything exciting happen?"

Alyssa replied: "Well, we did take a field trip to a place I had never been before. A Maker Faire."

Uncle Mikey responded: "Ah yes, I've been to a few of

those before.   What did you see?"

She responded: "Well, the best exhibit was probably the one with the video game designer.   We met a guy who works on the levels of video games. He helps create the levels in the games."

He asked : "Is that something you might want to do? Does it seem interesting?"

Alyssa answered: "Yeah, it seems super interesting, but I don't think I would be great at it. I'm no good at imagining, and what he did looks like you'd need a lot of imagination. Ms. Powers said I could get better at imagining anything, but I don't think she's right. I'm not especially creative, and that's me."

Uncle Mikey shook his head.   "Nah, I remember you being plenty creative as a toddler.   You can get better. Remember your great grandpa Gene? He figured out how to play accordion when he was in his fifties! But I know, I'm sure adults lecture you all the time about how you can be creative if you try."

He asked: "Anything else about the video game exhibit?"

Alyssa said: "Yeah.   When we finished talking to him, he said he was about to leave his job! He said he had plans to move to another state where he was going to work on laptops, but not on video games.   We didn't understand why he wanted to leave a job creating video games! That's what everyone wants to do!"

Her uncle replied: "Creating video games is absolutely something a lot of kids think about doing. And it's probably a neat job. It sounds like he had his fun, but I'm sure he has his reasons for leaving and starting another job."

Alyssa responded: "He did say something about moving to some place colder and wanting to try out another type of work."

Uncle Mikey said: "That happens. I'm sure you remember me telling you about my friend Mark I had worked with at NASA who decided to leave a few years ago. I'm sure he's doing what he thinks is the best for him. Anything else about the Maker Faire?"

She answered: "Yes! I forgot to tell you! Ethan and I are going to build a crane! It's kind of like the robot arm you are making for the Mars rover! We're going to get a kit!"

Her uncle laughed and replied: "I wish NASA had given me a kit!"

Alyssa continued: "Well I'm sure our kit isn't exactly a robot arm, but it does have an app on a phone where you can tell it where to go and when to go up and down! It comes in about two weeks. I guess we'll learn more about it when we actually see it."

Uncle Mikey replied: "Kits can be a lot of fun. I guess what I'm doing is kind of like a kit. Except mine is a million pieces and didn't come with instructions! Most of our projects are like that: lots of pieces, and we have to write the instructions."

Alyssa responded: "So you basically still play with LEGOS at work?

He laughed and replied: "Well, I guess you could kind of say that. But our LEGOS go to space!"

Alyssa laughed too: "I'm glad I have a kit!"

She asked her uncle: "So how is your project going? Is it ready to be sent to Mars?"

Uncle Mikey responded: "Not quite yet. We are still doing lots of final testing. There's a lot of things that could go wrong with how our robot arm is going to be used, so we are considering every possible way it could be used, writing tests for it, and seeing if it passes all the tests."

She responded: "So you fixed all the problems? Were there any of those 'root causes' you told me about?"

He continued: Indeed, we have found a lot of root causes of problems. And that's good. If all the tests passed on the first time, that would mean we didn't write good tests. Maybe you've seen the phrase: "'Failure is not an option'. It's on some NASA stickers I see at gift shops."

As Alyssa tried to recall the memory of the gift shop, her uncle surprised her when he said: "I don't like it."

Alyssa leaned her head to the side with a confused look. "You don't like what? The bumper sticker? You want failure?"

He laughed and shook his head. "Well, it's not anyone WANTS failure. The phrase is appropriate every now and then. It traces back to the late nineteen sixties, when NASA was sending the first humans into space. It was super important to not make big mistakes. They didn't want to lose anyone. There was almost no room for error. And I can understand that."

"But. There are plenty of goals of less consequence than putting humans in space. You HAVE to expect some failure. At least at first. You have to know the first few times, you are almost certainly not going to get it right."

"When we first design, we expect the first few rounds of testing to have some problems. That's how we work out the problems. Maybe you've heard of the phrase 'debugging' before? The word 'debugging' came from the early days of computers, when they would find actual bugs in the equipment! These days, we don't have real bugs, but we do have little problems we need to fix, and we call them 'bugs'. When we find and fix the problems, that's 'debugging.'"

Alyssa smiled and said: "Maybe you should get a Venus Flytrap? That eats bugs."

He laughed and responded: "Ha, that's not a bad idea. Maybe I should get one of those for my desk."

Uncle Mikey and Alyssa continued talking for a while. They chatted about other things: video games, family, and food. They finished chatting, and it was time for bed.

Alyssa kept thinking about "Failure is not an option". It was weird to hear Uncle Mikey say he didn't like the phrase.

CHAPTER 5

Several weeks passed.

When Alyssa walked into STEM class, she noticed the back table had a pile of boxes. It looked like the STEM kits. Alyssa joined the students as they craned their heads looking for their kit.

The bell rang to begin class.

Ms. Powers began with a smile: "Hello, Class!".

"I'm sure you are all happy to see me, but I can tell what you are actually excited about. Indeed, they have come in! You will be receiving and opening your kit today for the semester project with your partner."

Ms. Powers walked toward the back of the class where the boxes with the kits were stacked.

"Each team may now get their kit when I call their name. Each kit is labeled. Two at a time, please. You may open your kit after you get it, but please don't start putting it together yet."

As Ms. Powers called out the names of each group of students, Alyssa and Ethan anxiously waited. Ms. Powers FINALLY called their names.

Each group opened their kits and started sorting the bags with parts. Ms. Powers walked around with a camera and took pictures of all the parts of each kit.

As she spoke: "Class, these pictures are for me, but they can also be for you. Sometimes when you're building, you'll forget where a certain piece was or what it looked like, or whether you even had it! We can go back to these pictures later if we need to."

Ms. Powers continued: "Now. Anyone noticed anything missing in their kit?"

The class was silent until one of the students who was never afraid of speaking up, Danny, shouted: "The instructions!"

Ms. Powers smiled. "Indeed! Perhaps you will need these."

She winked as she held up a set of small books stacked together and said: "The instructions!".

She continued: "I took the instructions out before you opened your kits to remind you the instructions are usually important. With these kits, they are absolutely important. Are instructions always important?"

This sounded like a trick question. Teachers did this sometimes. No one raised their hand. Slowly, Madison, who was partnered with Danny, raised her hand. She answered: "Not always."

Ms. Powers exclaimed: "Correct!"

Ms. Powers continued: "Sometimes you don't need them. But sometimes you do. As us adults like to say, the answer is 'it depends'. Instructions for some things are absolutely necessary, like when you are building a car or making a table. But did you need instructions every time you played with LEGOs as a toddler?"

Alyssa thought back. She remembered building LEGOs when she was super young. Sometimes she liked to play with blocks to put together what she was imagining. She didn't always need instructions.

Ms. Powers walked around and passed out the instructions to each team.

As Ms. Powers walked, she said: "As you put together your kits, there will be times you'll have to figure out what to do on your own. There may be parts that break. There may be a piece that gets lost. But be patient with yourself as you put these kits together. Like putting together a puzzle, it may take a while, and you'll make lots of mistakes, but you'll eventually see the picture."

Alyssa was just glad to have the instructions back.

Ms. Powers finished passing out the booklets and made her way back to the front of the classroom. "These kits go together in a certain way. But that's not all you'll be doing. When you present your kits at the school Maker Faire, each team will also be showing what they added or changed on their kit. Your group will decide what to do. It should be something that makes your kit better. It doesn't have to be something too complex, but you need to add something of your own."

Alyssa was confused, and was about to ask where they should get the parts. But Ethan beat her to it. He raised his hand and asked: "What parts will we use for it?"

Ms. Powers smiled: "I don't know. Depends on what you make. Let your mind simmer on it."

Alyssa had no idea what to add. Her mind was blank, not simmering.

The teams went through their kits for the rest of the class. Madison and Danny had chosen the solar pow-ered car, which looked pretty cool. It was mostly as she had expected: it was like a monster truck with a crane. Alyssa started imagining how the pieces would go to-gether as she flipped through the instructions.

Alyssa became excited about getting the kit together. She told Ethan: "If it's cool with you I'm going to take home some of the kit today. I know it's the first day, but I'm excited. I'll ask Ms. Powers. I promise I won't break it or anything."

Ethan started to pack up his bag and looked up. "Um-mm...I guess. Just don't break anything. And don't do too much without me!"

Alyssa responded: "I won't, I promise. I'll get started on the base of the crane. I'll take home a bag and the instructions and see what I can do." She was gaining confidence in learning how to "think like an engineer".

After school, when Alyssa arrived at home, she carefully set down the parts of the kit she had taken home and the instruction booklet.

As she had put the parts on her desk, she heard her mom call from the next room: "Alyssa, can you keep an eye on Lincoln? He's in the living room playing."

Alyssa responded: "Sure, I'll check on him."

She walked by the gameroom to check on Lincoln and stopped by the kitchen to make herself a snack. Peanut butter and apple slices. Aaaand a few chocolate chips.

She finished her snack, and headed back to her room to start putting together the parts she had brought home.

When she got to her room, she saw Lincoln. He was near her desk.

Before she could say anything, she watched as Lincoln DUMPED the parts ON THE FLOOR.

"Lincoln! Those are for my project at school! You can't play with those!"

Alyssa started to gather the parts as Lincoln started to get upset. "But I want to play with them!"

Alyssa noticed one of his favorite toys, a truck that made sounds, was outside of his room. She pointed at the truck and said: "If you go play with your truck, I'll give you a snack!"

It worked. Lincoln went outside her room to start playing with the truck.

As Alyssa put the pieces on her desk, she noticed one of the wheels had been put on an axle.

Lincoln hadn't broken anything. She was still upset, but she realized he had even started to put it together. It wasn't perfect, but he apparently had the idea.

Alyssa looked at the instruction booklet still on her desk. Not with the pieces. Alyssa thought about what Ms. Powers had said about needing instructions. Sometimes you need them. But sometimes you don't. But she also didn't say anything about your six year old brother taking your things.

As promised, she got her little brother a snack and went back to her room. Knowing he wanted to see it, she said to him: "You can watch me put it together, but you can't touch the pieces."

Lincoln went in and out of her room a few times as she put it together. She was able to ignore almost everything as she put the base of the crane together. There were a lot of little pieces. It took her an hour, but she finished putting together all the pieces in one of the bags. She planned to bring it back to school the next day. Probably with the instructions.

CHAPTER 6

The next morning, Alyssa packed up the kit.

On her way to school, she saw a text from Ethan: "I hope you're not sick too. I feel blech. My mom had the flu, I hope I don't have it too. I may be out for a few days :("

As she walked into STEM class and passed the teachers desk, she did a double-take. She didn't see Ms. Powers.

She had a sub. And not a good one. Mr. Garvey.

She had had Mr. Garvey for math several times, and she wasn't a fan. Mr. Garvey was grumpy, unhelpful, and he always mispronounced Alyssa's name. He called her "Eliza."

As more students arrived, Alyssa headed towards the back of the class to get the rest of the Crane Kit. As she walked, she heard Mr. Garvey:

"Excuse me ma'am, where are you going?"

Alyssa replied "I'm getting the rest of my kit. We are supposed to work on them today."

Mr. Garvey responded: "Not today. Please take your seat."

"Great." mumbled Alyssa. She hoped he didn't hear her.

Milliseconds after the bell rang, Mr. Garvey addressed the class: "Take your seats everyone, take your seats. It's time for class. Come now, take your seats." He wasn't yelling, but it sure seemed like he was.

He continued: "Ms. Powers is out this week for a family matter. I will be your substitute until Friday. Today there will be a lesson and a quiz. So listen up. The video will last for thirty four minutes, and the quiz will begin precisely at ten minutes to the bell. Now let's begin."

Alyssa wasn't excited about the week anymore.

Mr. Garvey put on the video about the history of computers. It would have been fun to learn about, except the narrator had a way of making interesting topics not so interesting. The narrator's droning voice made her feel as though she was listening to a computer talk about computers.

Alyssa was halfway listening, but she kept getting distracted thinking about her Crane Kit. She was doodling pictures of how she thought it could work.

Her ears perked up when the video started talking about "punch cards". They were one of the first ways to create a large "program" for computers to run. She remembered one time her grandpa had talked about punch cards when he had been in college. In the nineteen seventies! She had known punch cards were old, but not that old!

CHAPTER 6

Alyssa switched between paying attention to the presentation and doodling in her notebook. She barely registered the presentation ending. Then she remembered. Quiz time. Wonderful. NOT! Mr. Garvey walked around and passed out a quiz to each student.

Alyssa looked at the first question: "What does the word ENIAC stand for?"

She had no idea. She remembered seeing that part of the video, but she didn't remember what it stood for. Maybe the E was for elephants? Definitely not. She left the answer blank, and moved onto the other questions. She knew some answers, but she guessed on about half. This may not be a grade she would be happy about.

The bell rang, and students walked past the teachers desk to hand in their quizzes. She stopped at the desk to ask her least-favorite substitute teacher: "Mr. Garvey, since we didn't get to work on our kits in class today, can I take different parts of it home? Ms. Powers said it was ok."

He didn't look up from the computer, but responded in his dull voice: "As long as Ms. Powers said it was ok, I suppose so."

She picked up another bag from the Crane Kit in the back, the instructions, and carefully put them in her backpack. After she picked up her belongings from her locker, she started the walk home. As she walked out the door, she saw Adelyn.

"Hey Adelyn!", Alyssa said to Adelyn. Alyssa had mostly forgiven her for not joining her in STEM class.

"Hey! How are you?"

Alyssa answered: "Well today, could have gone better. Pretty sure I failed a quiz. We had a substitute, and he wasn't the greatest."

Adelyn asked: "Mr. Garvey?"

Alyssa answered: "Yes. Mr. Garvey."

They both made faces at each other. They did not like Mr. Garvey.

Alyssa asked Adelyn: "So what are you doing after school today? Want to come over? I am working on my Crane Kit, and I'd love to show you what I'm working on. It's going to be a robot crane! It's going to be able to pick things up and set them down. And when we get it together, we can control it with a phone!"

Adelyn responded: "Ummm...well actually, I've got practice, so not today. Sorry."

Alyssa was disappointed.

"Oh, ok."

Alyssa tried to think about what they still had in common. They talked about Adelyn's birthday party a few weekends ago, where Adelyn's parents had rented out a roller skating rink. Alyssa remembered when she and

Adelyn would roller blade together. They remembered how they used to help keep each other from falling down, and how they used to skate around the neighborhood.

When the turn came for Adelyn to head to her house, they split up once again, and Alyssa continued home.

The next part of the Crane Kit to put together was the motor to make the crane turn from side to side. The motor went on top of the wheels she had put together the day before.

Today was one of the few days she didn't have any homework, so as soon as she got home, she emptied the bag out on her desk and flipped the instruction book to the pages she needed. She knew she couldn't do too much without Ethan, but she at least wanted to get started.

As she started to piece together the motor, she saw wires she was unsure what to do with. The instructions showed two wires connected to the battery, so she connected them. It seemed simple enough, but it wasn't working. She tried turning on the motor with the switch. Nothing. The motor wouldn't turn.

She kept looking at the instructions, wondering what she was doing wrong. After trying to figure it out for another thirty minutes, she became frustrated, and decided to take a break. So much for instructions.

She went downstairs, ate dinner, watched a show, and got ready for bed. She didn't say much at dinner. She hoped tomorrow would be better than the day she just had.

The next day was a little bit better. Not much, but some. Mr. Garvey was still going to be part of it, so THAT was not a plus.

As she arrived at class, she saw Ethan's empty desk. He must still be sick. She set down her bag and saw a simple sentence on the board: "Today you may work on your kits."

As soon as the bell rang, Mr. Garvey announced to the class: "Well, you saw the board. Today you may work on your kits." He sat down, not seeming excessively interested in anything except for what he was reading on his phone.

Alyssa pulled out the motor she had brought from home, hoping she could get it running today. She figured she could ask for help from Mr. Garvey, so she went to his desk.

She approached and asked: "Mr. Garvey, can you help me? I can't get my motor to run."

He responded with a disinterested voice: "Beats me. I don't know about motors. Didn't you already learn about all that? Were you not paying attention?"

Alyssa returned to her desk. Chalk up another reason to not like Mr. Garvey .

As Alyssa sat, she stared at the instructions and the motor that wouldn't run. She compared the instructions to what she had built. She must have looked at them a hundred times. Motor still wouldn't run.

She noticed Madison sitting at a desk over. She watched as Madison and her partner Danny continued to put together their kit. They had chosen a solar car, but it looked like it had motors too. It seemed like Madison was pretty smart, so Alyssa thought she might ask her for help. Madison was quiet, but she seemed nice.

Alyssa tapped Madison on the shoulder: "Hey, how's it going?"

Madison responded: "Pretty good, I guess. Our solar car is pretty cool."

Alyssa looked at their kit and agreed: "Yeah, that does look neat."

She hesitated. She picked up the motor in her hand to show it to Madison. Alyssa asked: "Hey can you help me? I can't get this motor to run."

Madison turned around to examine the setup on Alyssa's desk. Madison flipped the switch several times and watched a spectacular nothing happen.

Madison picked up the motor and the wires to the battery, turned it over and over, and announced: "Oh I see the problem."

Alyssa saw Madison do something to the wires and watched in amazement as the motor started to run and the crane arm started moving to the side.

"Wait, what? What did you do?", said Alyssa. "How did you do that?"

Madison responded: "The wires were backwards. I switched them. Looks like it's working well now. I think that's something called polarity. Not sure."

Alyssa smiled at Madison: "Thank you!"

Madison went back to her desk. Madison was quiet, but asking her for help had turned out well. Alyssa had a small reason to be optimistic about the week again.

Alyssa made it through the rest of week with her unfavorite Mr. Garvey, and once again, it was the weekend, finally!

The weekend was full of rain, so she stayed inside. As she laid down on the couch, feeling bored, she realized she hadn't talked to Uncle Mikey in a while. She texted her uncle: "Hey Uncle Mikey! Can we talk?"

Her phone rang a few seconds later. She answered. The camera pointed away from his face and seemed to fumble around a bit, but she eventually saw his face on the screen.

Alyssa started the conversation: "Hey Uncle Mikey! Where are you?"

Uncle Mikey responded: "Just living with grease and wires! One of the cables on my car battery is worn out, so I'm changing it."

Alyssa said: "If now's not a good time, we can talk later."

She watched as her uncle set down his phone and wiped his hands with some paper towels. "No problem. I could use a break anyways." He picked up his phone again and sat down. He wiped the sweat from his brow.

Alyssa replied: "Funny you are working on a battery. In my class, the battery for the motor was connected backwards, so the motor wouldn't run. But there's a smart girl in my class who figured out what was wrong. Once she swapped the wires around, it worked great."

Uncle Mikey responded: "Ah, yes, a common mistake when you are first learning about electricity. You have to have the polarity right, which is a fancy way of saying which direction the electricity is flowing."

Uncle Mikey asked: "So, did Ethan help you figure it out?"

Alyssa responded: "No, it wasn't Ethan actually. He was sick the last few days, he thinks he has the flu. A girl named Madison helped me. I had tried asking the teacher first, but he wasn't super helpful. Madison's parents have engineering jobs or something. "

Uncle Mikey replied: "That's great. Sometimes help comes from unexpected places."

Alyssa laughed and said: "Yeah, Madison is quiet and she doesn't talk much. I didn't know she even knew about motors."

Uncle Mikey asked: "So how's the rest of life? How are your other friends?"

Alyssa responded: "Well, Adelyn and I saw each other again this week. Which was good. I guess I'm mostly over being mad at her. I haven't hung out with her much ever since she started soccer. I asked her if she wanted to come over and see my Crane Kit, but she wasn't interested. She used to be one of my good friends."

Uncle Mikey responded: "Sometimes life doesn't have instructions, does it?"

Alyssa replied: "I guess not. I like STEM class, but Adelyn doesn't. And she's been my best friend forever."

He replied: "I remember in high school I was super into model trains. Almost none of my friends were. But I thought it was fun. I would save up money for engines, paint the buildings and the trees, and think of different areas for the trains to go through. It was fun. I remember wishing I knew other people who enjoyed it."

He kept talking: "I never found anyone in high school I could share it with, but eventually, I decided I could enjoy it by myself if I wanted to. Sometimes, no one else is going to be interested in your hobbies, and that's OK. I've even got a friend that does soap carvings for fun."

Alyssa answered: "Soap carvings? Yeah I don't think I'm into that. I guess you're right, but I miss having someone who enjoys all the same things I do."

Uncle Mikey responded: "What you are going through is tough. Sometimes I wish someone was around who would work with me on the car. And every now and then it happens, but a lot of times, it doesn't. Sometimes the fun is figuring out problems for yourself."

Alyssa asked: "So did you fix your car battery wires? Don't connect them backwards!"

He got up from his chair and answered: "No, I didn't connect them backwards! I've made that mistake before, never will again! Let's find out."

He took the phone and set it on the front seat of the car. She couldn't see him, but she smiled when heard when the car start.

CHAPTER 7

STEM class started off the next Monday much better than the previous week with Mr. Garvey. Both Ethan and Ms. Powers were back. Alyssa felt bad Ethan had been gone so long, but she was happy he'd get to start helping with the Crane Kit again. She had texted Ethan about Madison correcting the reversed wires.

When Alyssa looked at the teacher's desk, saw another adult off to the side of Ms. Powers. Ms. Powers began class with an introduction:

"Class, I'm happy to be back. I'd like you all to welcome Mr. Waller. Mr. Waller is Madison's dad, and will be talking to us about what he does for his job."

Ms. Powers motioned for Madison's dad to make his way to the front of the class. Alyssa saw he dressed the same way her dad did. She figured there was a standard dad uniform dress code or something.

Mr. Waller began his presentation: "So. Who wants to be a tractor software designer?"

No one raised their hand.

He asked again: "Really? None of you? Ok, I'll pick something you can probably relate to more. How about hackers? Anyone?"

A few hands hesitantly went up. Mr. Waller asked: "Excellent. Now, what can you hack?"

One student shouted out: "Video games." Another student said: "iPhones!".

Madison's partner, Danny, said: "Hackberry trees!". The class laughed. Danny was always trying to be funny.

Mr. Waller continued: "Well, let me start off with a bit of history about the old man you see in front of you. I went to college and got a degree in cybersecurity. After college, I enlisted in the Air Force, where I was placed in a group doing cybersecurity. I figured I would be doing hacking, right? My first task was to run test procedures other people had written. It was fun at first, but running other people's tests for a few months wasn't quite as exciting as I thought it might be."

"I'm sure you've seen hackers in movies. And maybe even heard about a few hacking incidents in the news. What I do is kind of like what you hear about, but not exactly."

He kept talking: "My job as a hacker was to make systems more secure, not to break into systems. And sometimes, my job was to look at simple things, like whether a door lock had been installed correctly.   But as I kept working, I realized what I enjoyed was figuring problems out."

He started to walk towards the whiteboard as he said "And that's why I work on the software for tractors."

Alyssa raised her eyebrows and looked at Ethan.

He continued his story: "After I had served a few years in the Air Force, I decided to look for a job outside of the military. I wasn't quite sure what type of job I wanted, but I knew I wanted something where I could solve problems. I realized it's what I liked."

"I applied for several jobs, and the one I accepted is the one I'm still working at today. My company designs tractors, and I lead a team that writes software for them."

"I'm sure you're wondering what software has to do with tractors. And at first, I did too. But when I looked under the hood at what tractors do, I found software in all kinds of places I did not expect. There is software to control how the engine runs. There is software to run the control panel. There is software that controls a GPS receiver. There is software to control when the tractor should lower and raise equipment."

"The software for tractors is like an engine you can't see. It's constantly running, and most of the time, it does what it is supposed to do. Except for the times when it doesn't."

"I'm sure you've all had times you've had to reboot a phone because it doesn't work right, am I right?"

A few in the class nodded their heads. Ms. Powers did too.

"When your phone doesn't work right and one of the

apps is acting strange, the app has probably run into a bug. A bug is a mistake in the software. Something the programmers didn't think about. And when you reset your phone, you put the software back in a good state, which allows it to run like you think it should."

"And sometimes there are mechanical 'bugs.'"

He pointed to the screen where Ms. Powers had pulled up his presentation. He used a laser pointer to show the tractor, except you could see inside of it. It was like having x-ray goggles.

"When we first started putting the GPS sensors on the tractor, we thought we had picked out a good spot for them to be mounted. We put them close to the screen that shows the driver their location. Makes sense, right? To put the sensor near where you'd use it?"

"On paper, our idea worked great. We had a plan. And we made a prototype of the console and bought a GPS sensor, did some testing, and we were making good progress. Next step was to test mounting the sensor and console on a tractor to see how it would fit. And that's when it wouldn't fit."

"The area we had planned on using for mounting the sensor was too small. We realized we had made a mistake, we had not communicated well with the other engineers responsible for designing the area for it to be mounted. They thought we were using a different sensor."

"So it was a mistake. But we fixed it. As a temporary

fix, we cut out the area for it to fit and did our testing. We finished the testing we needed to do and went back and refined our design."

"Simple mistakes like this happen all the time.   Talking with each other and making sure others are aware of your plans is tremendously important. If you don't make sure you are on the same page, you may find both of you have been reading a different book!"

Mr. Waller signaled to Ms. Powers he was done with the slides, and she stopped the presentation. Mr. Waller began passing around a few other parts he had worked on: a router he had done cybersecurity testing on, some of the other wiring parts of the tractor, and even one of the GPS sensors he had talked about.

He ended his presentation by saying: "When I started working with cybersecurity, I didn't know if I'd like it or if I could learn enough about it. But I realized what I liked was learning new skills and fixing problems. Some people may not call it hacking, but I do.   That's what I get to do every day, and I enjoy it.   And it's neat to think what I'm doing is helping farmers get food to families like mine."

As he gathered the parts he had passed around, Mr. Waller said: "Remember, I had no idea I would work on software for tractors even when I got my college degree. But here I am."

He packed up the last thing in his bag, smiled, turned to the class, and said: "Don't be afraid of what you don't know."

Ms. Powers asked the class to give him a hand. Mr. Waller packed up his things, thanked the students, and left the classroom.

Ms. Powers asked the class: "Well class? Tractor software? Fun?"

Alyssa raised her hand and said: "I think so. Not sure. It doesn't sound as exciting as making robots."

Ms. Powers responded: "Fair point, Alyssa. But, remember: a robot is just something you can program to move. And some parts of the tractor Mr. Waller talked about are parts programmed to move. So, technically, yes, it is a robot. A big robot. Not Godzilla size. But it's still big."

CHAPTER 8

On the Monday of the next week, Ms. Powers told the students they could again use their time in class to work on their kits.

Alyssa and Ethan had made more progress in the previous week. They had completed the crane motor, the wheels, and the base. The kit was starting to come together. But there was still a lot left: the hook, the connection from the hook to the motor, and the legs that helped hold the crane down. A picture of the completed crane kind of looked like a spider with legs.

Ethan asked: "Ok. What do we work on next?"

Alyssa responded: "Well the instructions don't say we have to do it in a certain order, but it does seem like the next thing to do is the crane arm. The long piece with the hook at the end. It's called a 'boom' or something."

Ethan replied: "OK, sounds good. Do we have all the pieces for it?"

They emptied out more bags. They found the plastic joints that would make up the arm, along with pins to keep each part connected, along with connector pieces for the bottom part of the arm, and a connector piece for attaching the hook at the top of the arm.

As they put the crane arm together, Alyssa remembered

Ethan didn't know Mr. Garvey had been the sub the week before.

Alyssa asked: "So, remember Mr. Garvey?"

Ethan: "Oh, yeah. I remember him. Didn't care for him." Ethan shook his head.

Alyssa responded: "Well he was our sub for a few days last week when you were sick."

Ethan responded: "Really? I had a quiz as a makeup assignment, but I didn't know we had a sub."

Alyssa replied: "Yeah. He showed a few presentations, and he gave us a little bit of time to work on our kits. But not much. I asked him a question about the battery and the motor, and he was super unhelpful. He looked at me like I was a moron and should already know the answer. But I think I had texted you that Madison helped out. She looked at the motor and saw the wires were backwards. We swapped the wires, and the motor started working."

Ethan responded: "Yeah, I've had Mr. Garvey for a few other classes. Sometimes he's in a good mood, but sometimes he looks at everyone like they should know the answers. Other times, you can tell he's in a bad mood."

Alyssa said: "Yeah, I hope we don't have him again. I'm glad Madison was able to help. She's pretty cool. Quiet. But cool. Super weird that her dad writes software for tractors."

Ethan smiled and said: "Yeah I know, right? Sounds like he should have a cowboy hat on when he's working at his computer."

After about thirty minutes of following the instructions for putting together the crane arm, they finished. It was time to try it out.

Alyssa said: "OK, well, I guess it's time to see if it works. Maybe we can find something for it to hook onto?"

Ethan found a paperclip and held it on the table. "Here. Try this. The hook should be able to pick this up no problem."

Alyssa picked up the crane arm and lowered the hook into the paperclip. She pulled it up.

Ethan said: "Well, we can officially pick up school supplies. How about something heavier?"

Ethan looked in his backpack and pulled out the keys to his house. "Here! Try these. These are heavier than a paperclip."

Alyssa unhooked from the paperclip and moved the hook toward the keys. She latched onto the keys, pulled, and…..it fell apart. The entire arm.

Alyssa asked: "How heavy are those keys? They must be like ten pounds or something! It broke the crane arm!"

Ethan said: "Well it does have a flashlight on it my dad

gave me, but they aren't really heavy. We must have not put something together right."

They picked up the instructions and re-read them and looked at the crane arm as they did. Everything looked fine. They double checked each piece.

Ethan said: "I don't see anything wrong. What should we do? Should we ask Ms. Powers?"

Alyssa looked at her watch: "No, we don't have time today. Only three minutes left in class. But I know what to do. I'll take a picture of what we put together, and I'll send it to my Uncle Mikey. I'll bet he'll know what's wrong."

Ethan replied: "I hope he knows. Cause I have no idea."

Alyssa snapped a few pictures of the crane arm she would text to Uncle Mikey. She and Ethan put away their kit as the class packed up their belongings.

As Alyssa lifted her backpack on her shoulder, she said: "I bet if I text him after school he'll respond before to-morrow. Hopefully I'll know what's wrong, and we can keep working on it."

They went their separate ways, and Alyssa started the walk home. As she walked, she texted her Uncle Mikey. "Hey Uncle Mikey! So we have a problem. We put to-gether the arm of our crane, and it picks up light things, but it breaks when we pick up anything heavy. Do you know what's wrong? Here are some pictures."

Alyssa attached the pictures, hit send, and finished her walk home. She kept trying to figure out what they did wrong. She was stumped.

That night, after dinner, she saw a text from Uncle Mikey. It said "Yes, I know what's wrong." But no other text than that.

She replied to him: "Well, what is it? What's wrong????"

Uncle Mikey texted back: "I will tell you, but not yet. If you still don't know what's wrong by tomorrow night, I'll tell you."

Alyssa was annoyed when adults did this. It was like when the teacher knew the answer they wanted students to give, but kept asking the question over and over even though no one knew what to say.

Alyssa decided to call him. He would tell her if she asked enough. He always wanted to help, right?

He answered: "Hey! You already figured it out?"

Alyssa responded: "No, I don't know the answer. That's why I asked you! You said you know the answer."

Uncle Mikey responded: "Yes, I do. I see what's missing."

Alyssa was getting upset. "So what's missing?"

Uncle Mikey responded: "There have been more times than I can count when I leave work with a problem I have no idea how to solve. And if I keep trying to force my brain to come up with an answer without giving it a break, it doesn't work. I have to give it time to rest. Sometimes I exercise, sometimes I sleep on it, sometimes I go eat a meal. Then I come back and look at it. If you don't know the answer by tomorrow evening, I'll tell you what I think is wrong."

Alyssa was a little less annoyed, but was still a little frustrated. "Allright, allright!", she said disappointedly. "But if I don't know the answer by tomorrow night, you promise you'll tell me? Promise?"

Uncle Mikey responded: "Absolutely. If you don't know by tomorrow night, yes, I'll tell you. Promise. I'll even give you a hint. Flagpole. That's my hint."

Alyssa asked: "Flagpole? That's it?"

He nodded his head: "Yep. That's my hint. Goodnight, Alyssa."

"Goodnight, Uncle Mikey. You better tell me tomorrow!"

After the call with Uncle Mikey, she decided to play her Nintendo Switch, and she asked her Dad to play with her. She always chose to be Yoshi and her dad preferred Donkey Kong. And even though her dad REALLY wanted to race on Rainbow Road, they stuck with Bowser's Castle and Coconut Mall. They played for over an hour. She played enough to forget about her problem with the crane.

The next morning, on her way into school, she started thinking about her crane arm again. As she walked towards the entrance of the school, she saw the flagpole at the front of the school. Then she remembered Uncle Mikey's hint.

She stopped and stared at the flagpole.

It hit her.

The string. They were missing the string. Like the rope on the flagpole.

She remembered on the cover of the kit there was a string attached to the top of the arm and went back to the base of the crane. Since they had only been using the arm without it attached to the base, they hadn't seen the part of the instructions about connecting the string. It must be the string.

When she saw Ethan in class, she said: "I think I know what's wrong."

Ethan asked: "Your Uncle Mikey told you? Awesome! What's wrong? What did he tell you?"

Alyssa replied: "He didn't tell me. He only gave me a hint. He did that annoying thing adults do when they don't want to give you the answer. He told me 'flag-pole' was the hint. But, I think I know what's wrong. I looked at the flagpole outside the school this morning and it reminded me we are missing the string. There's a string that goes from the top of the crane arm to the base. And the string helps it stay together when it is picking things up."

Ethan responded: "Let's try it."

Ethan and Alyssa found the string and the related pieces. It took some time to take apart put the crane arm back together, but after a few more minutes, they had the arm connected to the base, this time with the string.

Alyssa said: "Let's try the paperclip again, to make sure it still works."

Ethan moved the crane base and the arm together and positioned it over the paperclip. They hooked it in, and he pressed the button to pull up the paperclip.

Ethan said: "Ok, easy enough. Now let's try my keys."

Ethan put his keys on the table, and they positioned the crane hook into them.

They slowly lifted the hook on the crane, hoping it would not break. She closed her eyes as it started to pick up the keys. She waited to hear the sound of it breaking.

Alyssa slightly opened her eyes as Ethan lifted it. Ethan asked with his eyes closed: "Is it about to break?"

Alyssa looked and said "Nooo....I don't think soo....so far so good...."

Ethan kept lifting the crane hook, until it held the keys several inches off the desk.

Alyssa said: "It worked! It's fine now!"

They looked for other things to pick up. They tried picking up binder clips, binder clips attached to the keys, more paper clips attached to the keys, and anything else they could find that had a hook on it. It picked all of them up without a problem.

They were happy with themselves. They put away their kits for the day, and on her way home, Alyssa texted her Uncle Mikey: "I figured it out! We were missing the string! I still wish you would have just told me though!"

Uncle Mikey replied: "Well I guess I don't have to tell you tonight! Sometimes a good night's sleep and getting your mind off the problem can do a lot. I've got one right now I'm going to have to take a break from."

Alyssa responded: "Cool. Hope you figure it out."

Uncle Mikey responded: "I usually do. Just takes time."

CHAPTER 9

The Crane Kit now had wheels, a base, the crane arm, and a motor to lift and lower the hook.

It was time to make the Crane Kit turn. Like a fisherman turning to cast the rod, the kit had pieces to make the crane turn left and right, so it could pick up an object here and place it there.

Alyssa thought about Uncle Mikey's robot arm and how it would be picking up dirt. On Mars. Just like when she was small, and played in the sandbox. She had picked up dirt. But not dirt from Mars.

Alyssa and Ethan got out more plastic bags with the parts for making the crane turn left and right. There was another motor, some gears, a few other plastic pieces, and wires to connect the motor to the batteries.

Ethan pointed to the instructions, held them over a trash can, and joked with Alyssa: "I'm sure we won't need the instructions, right?"

Alyssa smiled and replied: "Don't even THINK about it. Sometimes you DO need the instructions. We're going to need them here."

The instructions said to attach the gears together inside a plastic housing. When the motor would spin, the gears would connect to each other, and the crane arm would turn left and right.

The gears were tricky to put together, and it took them a few times, but they knew the parts were in the right spot when they heard a satisfying "click" as the parts snapped together.

They were excited to see the crane arm move left and right. They connected the wires, not getting them backwards this time, and flipped the switch on the motor .

They heard a clicking. "Click-click-click", like a fast clock ticking.   But it wasn't moving.

Alyssa said: "What's wrong?   It's not moving.   Did we mess something up?"

Ethan replied: "Not sure. Turn off the motor."

Ethan turned off the motor, and they looked closer at the gears.   They searched and searched.   They looked for several minutes, until Alyssa chimed up with excitement:

"I found it! There's a little screw stuck in there. We must have dropped it."

Alyssa reached into the gears to take out the screw. It was stuck, so she pulled hard. She pulled even harder, until…..the screw came out.

Along with a piece of the gear.

She had cracked it.   She had CRACKED one of the

gears. It was the biggest gear on the motor.

She realized what she had done. "I broke it! That was so dumb! I can't believe I did that!"

Her face got red. Her hands got sweaty.

Ethan could see she was embarrassed: "Maybe Ms. Powers can fix it?"

Alyssa replied: "I have no idea. Maybe. I can't believe I broke that. That was so dumb. So dumb."

Alyssa wanted the class to be over. She wanted to crawl into a hole.

Ms. Powers had been walking around the class watching the students put together their kits.

Alyssa saw Ms. Powers walking the class complementing the other teams: "Nice job, Madison and Danny, your kit is coming along.   The solar car is going to be really neat."

Ms. Powers made her way down the rows, finally arriving at Alyssa's desk. Alyssa wished she could become invisible.

Ms. Powers asked: "Something wrong, Alyssa?"

Alyssa did NOT even want to tell Ms. Powers about the broken piece. But Ms. Powers was now standing over her, and Alyssa didn't have much of a choice. She felt like she had broken one of her mom's super expensive dishes and her mom was staring at her.

Alyssa looked down as she spoke. "You could say that. I broke a super important piece. I'm a disaster."

Ms. Powers smiled and said: "A disaster would be a hurricane. YOU are not a disaster! You've just got a broken piece."

Alyssa calmed down a bit since she saw Ms. Powers was still smiling. Some of the redness drained from her face. But she was still embarrassed.

Ms. Powers picked up the broken gear and tried to fit it back together. As she tried different ways to put it back together, she said to Alyssa: "You know how you get good at fixing, right?"

She gave the standard answer adults always wanted to hear: "Practice."

Ms. Powers smiled and said: "Yes, I suppose. That's what we teachers always say, right? Practice, practice, practice. And there's some truth to that. But I suppose what I mean is..."

Ms. Powers put her glasses back up as she set down the broken gear.

"It's good to mess up."

Ethan looked confused. He asked: "That's good? To mess up?"

Ms. Powers said: "Sometimes. Absolutely."

Ms. Powers continued: "It's hardly reasonable to expect that every time you work on something you're going to get it right the first time. Most things are much too complicated to get right the first time. When you start on projects knowing you're going to mess up a few times, it's easier. It's easier because you can forgive yourself when you make mistakes. And by forgiving yourself, you allow your mind to move on. And find solutions."

Ms. Powers squinted again and picked up the gear. "And it looks like the solution here is going to be to get a new gear. It looks like it has broken into several pieces, and it's going to be hard to glue. I'll look online shortly and see if I can find another."

Ms. Powers took the broken gear and continued walking around, watching the other students work on their projects.

"Well at least she wasn't mad," said Ethan.

"I know. That's good I guess. Imagine if it had been Mr. Garvey!"

Ethan frowned.   "THAT would not have been good."

Alyssa said: "Yeah, Ms. Powers is cool. I'm glad she didn't get mad. But I screwed up. I'm pretty mad at myself. I can't believe I did that."

Ethan replied: "But she said she should be able to find a

replacement. It'll be OK."

Alyssa replied: "Maybe. I'm done with the kit for today. I'm not in the mood to work on it. I'll probably break something else."

Ethan continued to look at the next steps for putting the rotation motor together, and Alyssa went back to her desk and pretended to read a book. She wanted to go home.

The bell rang, and Alyssa picked up her bag, and headed for the door. On her way out, she asked Ms. Powers: "Ms. Powers, were you able to find a replacement gear?"

Ms. Powers looked over her glasses at her computer monitor: "Well, the good news is yes, I did find a replacement gear."

"But the bad news is it's not available anytime soon. The website here says …. one week. But I'll order it today."

Alyssa's smile turned into a frown.

———————————————

On her way home, she texted Uncle Mikey: "Hey. I know I just bothered you about the project, but I need to talk to you again. I screwed up. I broke something in the kit."

Uncle Mikey responded faster than she thought he would: "Sorry. I'll call you tonight."

Later in the evening, Alyssa saw a FaceTime call from Uncle Mikey. She answered the phone but didn't say anything. He saw her sad face and asked: "Is this about the broken piece?"

Alyssa responded: "You guessed it. I've ruined our kit."

Uncle Mikey smiled and responded: "Ruining your kit would be running over it with a car. I'm betting you didn't run over it with a car, right?"

Alyssa smiled: "No. Didn't run over it with a car. Maybe I should though."

Uncle Mikey replied: "Go easy on yourself. It happens. Now what broke?"

Alyssa said: "One of the gears. In the part that connects to the motor to make the crane turn left and right."

Uncle Mikey responded: "Bummer. Was it plastic?"

Alyssa answered: "Yes. Plastic."

To her surprise, Uncle Mikey said: "That's great news."

Alyssa asked: "What do you mean? HOW on earth is that great news?"

He replied: "Because we can make another one."

Alyssa was confused. She asked: "Another one? Ms. Powers already looked online, and she said they have them, but it would be a week before it comes in."

Uncle Mikey replied: "The one I'm thinking of would be more like two days to come in."

He smiled as he got up from his chair and took the phone with him to his computer room. He flipped the camera on the phone around so he could show Alyssa what he was looking at.

Uncle Mikey pointed at a machine and said: "See this? This is a 3D printer. You've probably seen one I'm sure. I can make you a replica of your broken gear."

Alyssa replied: "That's great, Uncle Mikey. But you don't know what it looks like."

Uncle Mikey turned his camera back around so Alyssa could see his face: "I may not know yet, but I will find out soon. You're going to show it to me. Here. Let me pull up the website for this kit."

Alyssa heard a few clicks, and Uncle Mikey flipped the camera around again so she could see what he was seeing.

Uncle Mikey asked: "Is your Crane Kit this one here?"

Alyssa replied: "Yes. That's the one."

Uncle Mikey said: "Ok. Great. Now, let me find the parts list for it….. here it is. Ok, now looking for the left-to-right motor….there it is….and looking at the parts for it…..got it."

Alyssa said: "Got what?"

Uncle Mikey said: "A picture of what it looks like. Between this picture and a few others of it, I should be able to make another one on my 3D printer."

Alyssa asked: "Are you sure? You can do that?"

He replied: "We'll find out. I will look at the diameter of the gear, how many teeth it has, and how large the hole in the middle is. If I find out those dimensions, I can model it in a software program, and send it to the printer. I'll let it print overnight, and, just in time for breakfast, we should have a new gear."

Alyssa said: "But you live halfway across the country. How am I supposed to use it?"

Uncle Mikey replied: "Your mom forgot a few of your brother's clothes when she visited. Anyways, I've been meaning to mail them back. I'll put this gear in there with his clothes. I can mail it tomorrow, and it should be at your house in a few days."

For the first time on the call, Alyssa smiled. She said: "Thanks, Uncle Mikey. You're the best."

He responded: "Don't be so hard on yourself. If you keep going with STEM, you need to expect to make mistakes. You have to make mistakes so you know how to fix things when they break. You always do it better the second time. I've made a lot of mistakes when 3D printing!"

Alyssa replied: "I know, I know. Ms. Powers said the same thing."

He replied and winked: "Sounds like she's made plenty of mistakes too."

CHAPTER 10

The next morning, Alyssa saw a text from Uncle Mikey: "Hey. Still mad at yourself?"

Alyssa smiled and responded: "Kind of. But I guess it's not so bad since you are going to make us a new gear."

Uncle Mikey responded: "What's for breakfast?"

She wrote back: "Strawberry Pop Tarts. And my mom made me eat REAL strawberries too.", with an emoji of a strawberry.

Uncle Mikey responded with a smiley face emoji and said: "Food cheers me up sometimes. Have a good day at school. I'm going to be mailing your new gear today. Don't be too hard on yourself. Imagine yourself on Mars. Your problems can look pretty small when you're one hundred ninety five million miles away!"

STEM class was the same as it had been for the past few days. Ms. Powers was giving them time in class to work on their kits.

After the bell rang, Ms. Powers announced to the class: "Today is another day to work on your kits. Remember, there are only three weeks until the school Maker Faire!".

Alyssa and Ethan got back to sorting their bags to begin

putting together the next part. She tried not to think about the gear she had broken.

Ethan said: "Oh yeah, I guess we better start thinking about what we are going to do on our own for this?"

Alyssa replied: "On our own? What are you talking about?"

Ethan responded: "Remember? She said we have to do something to our kit that's not in the instructions. And it doesn't have to be too fancy, but something we add ourselves."

Alyssa responded: "Oh yeah. I have no idea what to do. Any ideas?"

Ethan responded: "Put a LEGO man on top? I've got nothing."

Alyssa laughed: "A LEGO man would be fun. But I'm betting that's not what Ms. Powers is looking for."

Ethan responded: "I don't know. Maybe paint it or something? Or decals? Teachers always love creative stuff."

Alyssa responded: "That might be cool. But I was thinking we should add something more STEM-ish. Like a light. I don't know. But do you get what I'm saying?"

Ethan said: "Yeah. We'll think of something."

They used the rest of the class time connecting the crane

arm to the electronics. They were able to put together the pieces they needed without having the gear that Alyssa had broken.

At the end of class, they put their kits back in the storage areas. Ethan said: "So I vote that tonight we try and think of what we could add to our kit. And I'll try to think of something better than a LEGO man."

On the walk home, Alyssa put her mind to work thinking about what they could add to the kit.   As she was walking, she heard an ice cream truck in the distance.

She knew what to do.

Hearing the ice cream truck reminded her of an electronics snap-circuit kit her parents had bought for her when she was in elementary.   It was a long time ago, but she remembered part of the kit was a sound machine. The machine connected to a battery and would play different songs. Simple enough. They could add the song and play it when the crane was going up and down. They'd have to press a button to turn it on, but Ms. Powers said it should be simple.

When Alyssa got home, she asked her mom: "Hey mom -- where is the electronics snap-circuit kit I used to play with? Remember? I was in second grade or something when I got it as a Christmas present."

Her mom looked at her and replied: "Hmmm… I'm not sure. I have no idea where it is. I might have to go through some boxes in the attic. What did you need it for?"

"Nothing. Just thought it could be fun to play with."

She'd look for it later. She wanted to take a break for now.

She went upstairs, slouched on the couch, and turned on the TV. As she was watching a show, she heard Lincoln playing in the next room. She knew he was playing with trucks. She could hear the electronic rumbling of the pretend engines on the trucks.

She sighed. The songs of the snap circuit kit would have been perfect.

But after the show ended, she had an idea.

Maybe she could use one of Lincoln's toys? They make sounds.

She went downstairs and asked her mom: "Hey can I have one of Lincoln's toys?"

"Why do you want Lincoln's toys? What are you going to do with them?"

Alyssa replied: "Can I have one of his toys that makes a sound? I need to use it for a project at school."

Her mom raised her eyebrows: "I suppose you could borrow it, sure."

Alyssa responded: "Well, I may need to take it apart."

Alyssa's mom looked concerned. "What exactly are you looking to do here?"

Alyssa said: "I need the parts that make the sound. I'm going to put it on our Crane Kit for STEM class. Ms. Powers said we have to add something of our own, and I thought we could add a sound one of his toys makes."

Her mom thought for a few seconds and said: "Well, I do have a box of toys Lincoln hasn't played with in a long time. Maybe there's something in there. Go look in Lincoln's closet. In the corner, there's a blue plastic box. See what you can find."

Upstairs, in Lincoln's closet, Alyssa opened the box and started to go through the toys. She saw some of the old ones she used to play with: trains, animals, a kitchen set. She kept digging, and finally, at the bottom, she found almost exactly what she was looking for.

It was a toy snowman that played a song. It had two buttons. One of the buttons would play "Rudolph the Red Nosed Reindeer", and the other button played the song "Jingle Bells".

She figured she might be able to get the parts that made the sound out of the snowman. She took the snowman down to the garage, and found some tools at the work-bench.

She had never done this before. Taking apart a toy. Where was she even supposed to start? With a hammer? She figured the worst that could happen is she would break it. And she had already told her mom she needed the toy.

She looked at the bottom of the toy snowman and saw several small screws. She figured it would be a better place to start than a hammer.

She found a small screwdriver, and removed all the screws she could find. After removing them, she tried to pull off the plastic piece on the bottom. She pulled almost as hard as she could, and it still wasn't coming off.

She looked closer, and realized there was one screw she had missed. She removed the final screw, and the plastic bottom popped off.

Underneath the plastic bottom were all kinds of parts she had never seen in a toy before. She recognized the batteries, but she saw all kinds of different colored wires, green boards, and a lot more screws.

She looked for the wire that came from the two buttons, and after some searching, found them. She pressed both of them. They still worked. She smiled when they still played the songs. She hadn't broken anything yet!

Next she tried to figure out how she could get the parts out.

She saw more screws holding down the parts that made the sounds. It looked like a big black dot on a green board. She guessed it was the speaker. After hunting for all the screws she could find, she finally removed the last one. She reached down, and started to pull out the board.

It wouldn't budge. She pulled even harder. Finally, it came out.

And it came out with a loud snap.

She saw some of the plastic had broken, but the wires had not. She had no idea if the wires were important for it to make the sound or not.

She closed her eyes, and pressed a button to see if it still played the song. She heard the glorious tune of Rudolph The Red Nosed Reindeer.

She breathed a sigh of relief. They still worked like they did before.   She had gotten lucky. She broke something, but she still got what she needed.   Sometimes breaking things isn't bad, after all.

CHAPTER 11

"Ethan, it's perfect!"

It was the first thing Alyssa said to him when they met up in class.

"What are you talking about? Perfect for what?"

"The addition! The thing we are going to add to our Crane Kit!"

Ethan replied: "Oh yeah. I'm glad you came up with something, because the only idea I had was to add a Bob the Builder figure to it."

Alyssa hurriedly pulled out the parts. "See? This is something I took out of one of my little brothers' toys. When you hit the button, it plays 'Rudolph the Red-Nosed Reindeer'. It's a Christmas toy."

Ethan laughed, looked closer, and said: "Ok, kind of weird, but I guess it works. How did you get it out of the toy?"

Alyssa said: "Well I looked at the bottom and saw some screws. I took all the screws out, and the speaker and the button were right there together, along with a battery.   I took it out, and it worked!"

Ethan inspected it closer, and said "Nice job. We can

mount this right on the top." Ethan set the part down on Alyssa's desk.

Ms. Powers stood up to greet the students. "Hello class! Now, You know me as the teacher for this class. But, today, I'm happy to announce that you'll be the teacher. "

"Today, you won't be working on your kits. Instead, you will be working with fifth graders from the elementary school that's across the street."

Alyssa wondered why she had seen a line of elementary school students in the hallway. She figured it was a field trip or something.

Ms. Powers continued: "The fifth graders are here because next year, most of them will be coming to this middle school, so we will be teaching them about what to expect. Your job will be to explain one of our recent lessons to the fifth graders you are assigned to."

Alyssa got a bit nervous. She hoped she remembered something enough to be able to teach it. She searched her mind for the recent lessons they had had. Electricity? Computers? They had recently learned some about chemistry. Maybe chemistry?

Ms. Powers announced: "The lesson you will be teaching the fifth graders about today is computers. Remember recently we covered the basics of computers, and you remember the video with Mr. Garvey. I'll be handing out some papers to help jog your memory."

Ms. Powers walked around to pass out the papers.

"Now remember. You were a fifth grader last year, and you didn't know nearly as much as you do now. Keep it simple. Simple concepts are necessary not because they are not smart, but because they haven't learned about them yet. When you don't know about something. It doesn't matter if you are a rocket scientist or put together flower arrangements, you have to start with the basics. Simple."

Ms. Powers said each kit team would be paired with one elementary student for the class. Alyssa was a bit relieved she'd have Ethan to help her.

Ms. Powers opened the door and asked the teacher of the fifth graders to lead them into the room. "Class, please welcome these fifth graders to our classroom. Please show them what they have to look forward to if they take a STEM class here."

The fifth grade teacher greeted the class and started reviewing a list Ms. Powers had in her hand. Each fifth grade student was pointed towards a pair of her students.

A fifth grader started walking towards Alyssa and Ethan. She seemed shy.

Ethan saw she looked shy so tried to be friendly. "Hi! My name is Ethan. We are the sixth graders who will be telling you about our class today."

Alyssa gave a big smile and said: "Hey! I know you! You are Adelyn's sister! Hi Sophia!"

Sophia smiled for the first time and said: "Hi Alyssa!"

Alyssa said: "Well, Ms. Powers said we are supposed to talk to you about computers and our class."

Sophia asked: "Yeah, I think I might like it. So what do you do here? Is it fun?"

Ethan replied: "Yeah, it's pretty cool. We learn about engineering and science. And we build projects too."

Ethan looked at the back of the room, where the kits were stored. He squinted as he pointed his finger towards the end of one of the tables.

Ethan said: "See the kit that looks like a crane? That's ours. Alyssa and I are making it together. It's like a LEGO kit, but not exactly LEGOs. It has electronics and a crane that goes up and down. Oh, and it moves on wheels too! We'll show you the kit before you leave."

Sophia asked: "Is it hard?"

Alyssa said: "Yes, sometimes. It's hard when we don't know how to do something. Or we mess something up. But once we learn how to make it work, it's not so bad. It's fun."

Ethan handed her one of the papers Ms. Powers had passed out. As he gave Sophia the paper, he said: "So our teacher said we are going to teach you about what we learned about in a lesson."

Sophia took the paper and saw it was about computers.

She asked: "I've had a few computer classes in elementary, but they mostly teach us how to type and use the Internet. I want to understand how a computer works. Like what's actually going on inside?"

Alyssa hesitated. The paper they had was about the history of computers and famous people, but not about the guts of a computer. Alyssa tried to think of how to answer. It was a tough question.

There was a laptop on the desk beside them.

Sophia pointed at the laptop and said: "Like this one here? How does it work?"

Alyssa was hoping Ethan would jump in.

He did, and started with: "Well, it runs software and the software draws graphics on the screen."

Sophia asked: "How does it do that?"

Ethan answered: "There are electronics inside to turn the graphic drawings into screen colors."

Sophia asked: "How does it do that?"

Alyssa remembered her little brother sometimes endlessly asked "Why?" to her parents. She found it annoying, but she had to admit she understood why he did it. He was just trying to understand.

Alyssa remembered one of the things Ms. Powers told them about how computers work. She said to Sophia:

"Well, you know how cars do what you tell them, right? The driver tells it to turn with the steering wheel, and makes it go faster with the gas pedal, and stops with the brake pedal."

Sophia nodded her head, but asked: "Sure, but what does that have to do with a computer?"

Alyssa responded: "Well, Ms. Powers taught us computers are kind of like a car. When you give it 'input', which is kind of like steering the wheel, then the computer does what it's programmed to do, like a car turning. When you move the mouse or type on the keyboard, the software sees that you typed on the keyboard or moved the mouse, and it figures out what it should show on the screen."

Alyssa was a bit shocked this had come out of her mouth. Some of Ms. Power's lessons had apparently sunk in.

Alyssa's explanation had started to jog Ethan's memory, and he joined in: "I know. You know the buttons at the front of the car to change what music you can listen to? You can hit next and pause and change the volume? Ms. Powers told us those are computers too. So when you hit pause, the software in the computer stops playing music on the speakers."

Alyssa chimed in: "I guess a laptop is kind of like that. There's lots of buttons, right? When you press the buttons, the software decides what to do. Like when you type a website name and click Enter, the software brings up the web page. It downloads it from the Internet. Or something like that. We haven't learned too much about anything besides that."

Sophia responded: "So a computer isn't just a laptop?"

Ethan replied: "Ms. Powers said there are computers in a lot of places. She said that cell phones are computers. And I guess it makes sense. We tell the software what to do when we touch on different places on the screen. Touching the screen is like clicking the mouse on a computer."

Sophia said: "So do you take them apart or anything?"

Alyssa said: "No, we haven't done anything like that. But, let me show you something."

Alyssa reached for the button and the speaker she had brought from home and put it on the desk.

Alyssa pointed at the button and speaker and said: "I'm not sure if this is a computer or not, but Ms. Powers said these green boards are inside of them sometimes. See, check this out."

Alyssa pressed the small black button on the green electronics board, and the speaker played "Rudolph the Red-Nosed Reindeer".

Sophia said: "That's so cool! Christmas music! Where did you get that?"

Alyssa replied: "This is from one of my little brothers old toys. Our teacher said we had to add something extra to our kits on our own, and this is what we are going to add. When the crane on our kit goes up and down, we'll press the button, and Rudolph will cheer us on."

Sophia asked: "Can I try?"

Sophia hit the button and heard the song. She smiled and pressed it again.

Sophia asked: "That's cool. So can I see more of the crane thing you are building?"

Ethan and Alyssa walked with Sophia to the back of the class where they stored their kit. They showed Sophia the parts they had put together, and what they still had to add.

They looked at the kits until only a few minutes of class were left.

Ms. Powers said: "Okay students, time to let the fifth graders get back to their school tour!"

Alyssa and Ethan returned to their seats, and Sophia started to gather her belongings. As she stood up, she looked towards Adelyn and Ethan: "Thanks for showing me all this. It's pretty cool. I may want to take this class next year."

———————————

On her way home, far up ahead of her, Alyssa saw Adelyn walking with a group of friends. They weren't very close, so she decided not to try and catch up.

She was fine walking by herself for a little while. She didn't mind.

CHAPTER 12

It had been three days since Uncle Mikey said he was going to send the 3D printed gear Alyssa needed for her crane kit.   She was getting anxious.

After dinner, she saw a text from Uncle Mikey:

"Hey! The package I sent to your house should be there. Hope the gear fits!"

Alyssa immediately asked her mom: "Did we get any packages today?"

Her mom replied: "Hmm…yes. There was something your dad had said he picked up at the mailbox. Not sure what it was."

Alyssa replied: "It's got to be the package Uncle Mikey sent to me! A part for my crane kit.   Do you know where the package is?"

Her mom answered: "I haven't seen it around the house, so I'm guessing it's still in his car. Maybe there?"

Alyssa ran to the garage. Her dad's car was nowhere to be seen.

She went back inside. "Dad isn't here. Do you know when he's coming home?"

Her mom replied: "Oh yeah -- he went to the store to pick up a few things. He also has to run an errand after that. He may not be home until late."

Alyssa responded: "But I NEED that package! I have to have it!"

Her mom replied: "Honey, you'll get the part. You can get it out of dad's car tomorrow before he goes to work."

She stayed up until nine thirty, when her mom told her she had to get to bed. She had no desire to go to bed.

Alyssa said: "But mom, I REALLY want to see the part. Dad will be home soon, right?"

Her mom replied: "Probably. But you'll see the part in the morning. What's the big hurry?"

Alyssa frowned and said: "It's for fixing a part I broke in STEM class. I'm going to be anxious until I see it."

She reluctantly went to bed, and didn't sleep well.

The next morning, as she stumbled out of her bed, within a millisecond of her feet hitting the floor, remembered she needed to find the package.

She ran downstairs and saw the package on the counter. She tore it open and pulled out a few of her little brother's shirts. She saw it. A plastic bag with gears in it. She opened the plastic bag, found two identical gears, and found a note from Uncle Mikey: "Hope it fits! I printed two just in case. Mistakes happen!"

She slipped the plastic bag into her backpack.

When it was time for STEM class, she ran down the halls during the passing period. She arrived at the classroom before anyone else. She took out one of the gears from the plastic bag and carefully tried putting it in. It snapped into place. It was a perfect fit. She took a picture and texted it to Uncle Mikey.

Ethan walked in the class, and saw Alyssa in the back. Alyssa pointed to the gear and said: "Hey look! My uncle printed a replacement gear, and it fits perfectly!"

Ethan inspected the gear: "Awesome!"

Ms. Powers asked the students to take their seats and began the class.

"Class, we are only two weeks away from our own Maker Faire, where you will present your projects. The Maker Faire will not only be our school, but will include several middle schools from around the area."

"Like most events you are used to, there will be judges. They will select and present awards to the three most impressive projects."

"But, the judges will not just be looking at how your kit came together. They will also be judging a video. I've recommended to the judges that they grade based on a video of you and your partner explaining the kit, and they have agreed to this."

The class was surprised. Alyssa had braced herself for hearing about making a poster board, like they would for a science fair. She had made videos with her friends before, but never one explaining something. She and Ethan looked at each other.

Ms. Powers walked around the class and passed out pieces of paper. "This is the assignment. Tomorrow, we will be using a camera to take a video explaining how your kits work. This will be the submission to the Maker Faire for the judges."

She continued: "Your assignment for today, and your homework for tonight, is to write out what you are going to say in the video. Look at the different parts of your kits, decide who is going to talk about what, and make notes and practice your explanation. Please be ready to record tomorrow. I know this is short notice, but you will have all of the class to work on it, and each of you only needs to talk for one minute. Make it simple and to the point."

The students started chattering. Tomorrow was AW-FULLY short notice. Ms. Powers was usually reasonable, but Alyssa silently decided she didn't like Ms. Powers today.

Ethan said: "Ok. How about I'll explain the base and the wheels, and you explain the motor and how the crane moves up and down."

Alyssa nodded her head. Ethan started to write down notes about how to explain his parts. Alyssa tried to write, but the ideas weren't coming. She hadn't slept well the night before. Maybe she would feel better after school.   She spent most of the rest of the class doodling on her notes, not writing any ideas down.

Before she knew it, Ethan said: "Ok, I've got mine. I'll practice tonight."

Alyssa snapped up. She had almost nodded off. "Oh, OK. Yeah. Sounds good. I'm not feeling too awake right now, so I'll come up with my notes tonight and practice."

The bell rang.

Ethan said: "Sounds good. See you tomorrow!"

On the walk home, Alyssa tried to roll around ideas in her mind, but she was too tired to think. She wished she'd been more awake to work on it with Ethan during class. As she walked through the door of her house, Alyssa heard her mom: "Hi Alyssa -- please get your homework done soon. We are leaving in one hour."

"Where are we going?"

"To your dad's softball game and a pizza place with his team."

Alyssa remembered these games. The pizza place was fun. They had an arcade. They had stayed so long last time she fell asleep on one of the benches.

Alyssa remembered she had math homework, completed it quickly, and grabbed a snack. She had been tired, and she figured she deserved to sit down and watch some TV.

She watched a show and heard her mom call from downstairs: "Alyssa, time to go! Please grab your jacket and water bottle! We are leaving in five minutes!"

Alyssa grabbed a jacket, a water bottle, put on her shoes, and got in the car.

The softball game was fun. Her mom bought nachos, and she saw her dad make a big catch. The pizza place was fun too. She played some games with kids of the other people on her dad's softball team.

It was late when her family left. Alyssa fell asleep on the way home. They arrived at their house, and Alyssa shuffled off to bed, her eyes barely open.

As soon as Alyssa sat down in Ms. Powers class the next day, she had a sinking feeling in her stomach.   She had forgotten. She had forgotten about her assignment. She had made no notes about what to talk about in their explanation video. Zero.

Ethan walked in and said: "Hey Alyssa! Ready to be a YouTube star? I've got my notes for the video."

Alyssa turned red, and replied: "Ummmm...yeah....I'm not exactly ready to go."

Ethan asked: "What do you mean? Not ready for the

video?"

Alyssa replied: "No…..I'm not…. So we had a thing with my dad's softball team last night, and I didn't make any notes about what to talk about. I'm super sorry. I can't believe this. I should have remembered."

Ethan didn't have time to react, because just as Alyssa finished speaking, they heard Ms. Powers begin the class.

Ms. Powers said: "Ok, class! Time to be a star! We need to get started so we have time for everyone. First up for the video recording will be Ethan and Alyssa. Please grab your kit, and bring it up to the front of the class."

Alyssa's hands were sweaty. She had no idea what she was going to talk about.

Since Alyssa seemed frozen in her chair, Ethan grabbed their kit from the back and made his way toward Ms. Powers. Alyssa forced herself out of her chair and walked slowly towards the front.

Ms. Powers directed them to the two seats she had set up by the camera. The setup looked fancy: there was a tripod, a microphone with a fuzzy thing on it, and a flip-out screen on the camera.

As she prepared to record, she gave instructions:

"Ok. So, I'll point at you when I start recording. And both of you will take turns using your notes to explain the parts of the kits you decided on. Ethan, why don't you go first."

Ms. Powers hit record, pointed at Ethan, and he started his explanation. Alyssa didn't hear a thing. She was frantically searching her mind for what to say. It was like trying to look for a lightswitch in a dark room.

In what seemed like no time at all, Ms. Powers pointed to Alyssa, and mouthed the words: "Your turn."

Alyssa stared into the camera. She started to open her mouth several times, but no words came out.

After ten seconds, Ms. Powers hit pause on the camera and asked: "Is everything OK Alyssa?"

Alyssa tried to think of an excuse for why she wasn't prepared. She figured she could make something up, but she didn't think Ms. Powers would believe her. But if she told the truth, she'd be OK, right? Ms. Powers was nice, right?

"I forgot. I didn't make notes on what I was supposed to say. I was at this thing with my family last night. And I forgot. I'm so sorry. Can we do it tomorrow?"

Ms. Powers said: "I'm sorry, Alyssa, but no, we won't be able to do it tomorrow. We have another lesson planned, and I have to return this microphone and camera setup to the technology department."

Alyssa felt her stomach sink even lower.

Ms. Powers continued: "However, I will give you an

opportunity. If you and Ethan would like to, you can do the video tonight. You may take your kit home, and re-cord a video using a phone. If you turn it in tomorrow, it will not be counted as late."

Ms. Powers pointed at the next two students to record the video, and motioned for them to come up. She asked Alyssa and Ethan to return to their seats.

As they walked back, Alyssa could tell Ethan was upset. He hadn't said anything.

She hesitantly asked: "Soo….this afternoon? Can we record the video after school? Since Ms. Powers said we have to both be in it?"

Ethan was silent.

He finally replied. "I guess."

"I'm super sorry Ethan. I just plain forgot. I should have remembered. But we can take care of it."

Ethan was angry. With clenched teeth, he said: "I don't have any other homework and I was going to play basketball with some friends after school. And I don't even know if my mom can take me to your house. I was ready. Why weren't you ready Alyssa?"

She started to get angry. "Look I forgot, OK? I'm sorry! What else do you want me to do?"

Ethan put up his hands: "OK, OK, calm down. I don't want you to get upset about it. I'm just a little frustrated.

I wanted to hang out with my friends."

After a deep breath, Alyssa said: "I'm sorry. I'm mad at myself. Do you want to come over after school? We can record the video. And we can also play around with the app on the phone that controls the crane! Remember? We haven't used it yet."

Ethan's frown cracked a millimeter toward a smile when he remembered the app. "Oh yeah! I remember that! The app that moves the wheels and controls the crane, right? We downloaded it, but we can use it since it's all together!"

Alyssa replied: "Yep, that's the one." She was glad she had remembered to tell him about the phone app. He seemed less upset.

Ethan said: "Ok, hopefully it won't take too long. You promise you'll be ready, right? I'll ask my mom if I can come over."

Alyssa nodded her head: "Yes, absolutely. I'll be ready. I promise. I'll be ready."

She was thankful for a second chance.

CHAPTER 13

Alyssa carefully walked home with the boxed up Crane Kit as fast as she could; she wanted to make sure she had plenty of time to come up with what she would say in the video.

She took a seat at her dining room table. As she started jotting down ideas, she saw a text from Ethan:

"My mom said she can bring me over. See you in about twenty minutes."

Alyssa continued making notes, alternating between writing and looking at the crane kit on the dining room table.

As she walked around the table to get a look at it from another side, she saw Lincoln playing in the corner. She saw a few Magic School Bus books on the floor.

She couldn't shrink down to a Magic School Bus the size of a fly, but she could imagine she was a fly.

She tried to imagine going inside the crane. She started at the hook. She imagined the weight pulling on the hook, then on the string. And then the string to the pulley. She thought about the pulley the string went over, then the long "boom", which had to be extremely strong so the weight of what it picked up wouldn't snap the boom. The string then traveled to the motor, which also had a pulley on it. She imagined being part of the string being wrapped around the pulley as the motor turned.

Her imagination was interrupted by the doorbell ringing. She welcomed Ethan in.

"Hey. Ready to do this?"

Alyssa said: "Definitely. I've got some good ideas now about what to talk about. Give me a few minutes to finish up my notes on it and I'll be ready. In the meantime, there's some lemonade and cookies in the kitchen.

Ethan set his bag down and helped himself to the snacks in the kitchen. As he ate, he opened up his phone and pulled up the app to control the crane.

After finishing eating, Ethan joined Alyssa to the dining room with the crane, and flipped the switch on the electronics box to ON. He started to experiment with it going back and forth and the crane going up and down.

Alyssa's brother, Lincoln, watched Ethan and put his head up on the table.

Lincoln pointed to the corner of the room and said "Make it pick up animals!"

Alyssa's mom was passing the dining room when she heard Lincoln. Her mom smiled and said: "Oh he must be talking about the crane game we saw at the pizza place after your dad's softball game. Remember the game where you could try to pick up and win an animal?"

Ethan asked Alyssa: "Hey can we try to pick up one of the animals? Just for fun? It may not work, but I'll bet your little brother would think it's awesome."

Alyssa replied: "Sure. Lincoln, can we try to pick up one of your animals?"

Lincoln looked especially happy and went to the basket of stuffed animals. He returned with a stuffed squirrel with a bandana on it. He gave it to Alyssa.

Alyssa looked at it with Ethan. She said: "Maybe we can try to pick it up with a bandana?"

Ethan said: "Hmmm…I'm not sure it will work. The bandana doesn't have a great spot to put the crane hook around."

Alyssa said: "Hang on. I'll be right back."

She went out to the garage and the tool bench. Her dad had taught her how to use tie wraps before. Tie wraps were like flexible plastic zippers. She thought one may help in picking up the squirrel.

She came back and said to Ethan: "Here. Let's try this. I'm going to put the tie wrap around the bandana to make a loop. Then we'll have a good place to pick it up from."

Alyssa positioned the tie wrap, pulled it tight, but not too tight. She still wanted a loop to pick it up by.

As she positioned it under the crane, she said to Ethan: "Ok. Let's try it."

Ethan used the app on his phone to lower the crane. The hook moved closer to the loop on the tie wrap, and Alyssa positioned the squirrel a bit so the hook could grab the loop. She asked Ethan to hit the button to pull up the crane.

The squirrel started to rise in the air and her little brother started clapping and said "Yay! It's picking it up! It's picking it up!"

It made Alyssa happy to see her little brother so excited.

Alyssa said to Lincoln: "Ok Lincoln. We have to use our crane for school, but we can play later, OK?"

Lincoln asked, "More animals?"

She smiled and said: "Yes, more animals later."

Lincoln went back to playing with his toys, and Ethan put the Crane Kit back onto the table.

Alyssa said: "Ok, let's record our video. I've got a stand I'll put my phone on. And you can go first. And this time, I'll be ready."

Alyssa made sure the camera could see the crane kit and their faces, and hit record.

They introduced themselves and their project to the

camera.

Ethan looked at his notes.

"The wheels you see here snapped together like a LEGO set. You can't see it, but there is a frame holding the wheels together. Before you put together the crane and the wheels, it looks like a car would if you took the engine and the doors off. It's almost flat."

He continued:

"After the frame and the wheels were together, we had to connect the box that holds the electronics on top of the frame. But before we mounted the electronics, we had to make sure the motor and the battery were hooked up correctly."

He tilted the crane so the phone could see the electronics from a better angle. Ethan pointed out the connections to the battery and how the motor connected to the string. He explained how it was a pulley you didn't need to turn yourself. It was like an automatic fishing rod: the motor took care of reeling in and letting out the line.

Ethan explained a few more parts of the base, and said: "And now, my partner, Alyssa, is going to explain the top part of the kit."

Alyssa took over: "The crane part starts with the hook. The hook is like any hook: it helps grab the thing you want to lift. Then, when the hook has a good grip on the thing you are picking up, you can command the motor to turn with an app on a phone, and the crane starts moving up."

She pointed for Ethan to move the crane hook up using the app on his phone.

As it went up, she explained: "Ethan used his phone to tell the crane to go up. On his phone, he hit an area of the screen, which told the software to send a command from his phone to the electronics on the crane kit, which told the motor to go up, when pulled on the string, which moved the hook up."

She asked Ethan to press the button to move the crane down. Ethan pressed the button.

As the crane moved down, she explained: "When he hit the button to make it go down, pretty much the same thing happened, except the motor runs in reverse. Instead of pulling the string in, gravity pulls the hook down and the motor lets the string out."

They finished up the video by showing the app on Ethans phone to the camera so their audience could see how he had been using it for control.

They finished with "Thank you!"

Alyssa clicked the button to stop recording.

Alyssa said: "Ok, I think we've got it. I'm sorry I wasn't ready. I was anxious and I couldn't even think when I was in there. I feel better now. I barely had to look at my notes."

Ethan replied: "That's alright. We got it done now."

Alyssa responded: "I'll take care of sending the video to Ms. Powers. Thanks for coming over."

Ethan replied: "Cool. I'm going to chill with some friends and play basketball. My mom is still waiting outside. See you tomorrow."

Alyssa walked Ethan out and went back to her phone. She uploaded the video to her school account and shared it with Ms. Powers.   She also sent the video to Uncle Mikey and a text message: "We had to make a video for class where we explain how our kit works. Thought you might want to see it!"

She tapped send, put her phone back in her pocket and put the Crane Kit in a safe place, then took her things upstairs.

She started reading a book assignment for her English class. She was interrupted by a notification on her phone. It was from Ms. Powers.   The message read:

"Looks good! Glad you were able to get it done today."

Alyssa smiled. She had made a mistake, but it wasn't so bad. She had fixed it.

CHAPTER 14

On Friday night, Adelyn texted Alyssa.

"Hey! I know it's been a while since we hung out. Want to come to my soccer tournament tomorrow at ten o'clock? You can come with my family and you can join us for lunch after the games."

Alyssa was surprised Adelyn had texted her. It had been a while. And she didn't have anything better to do on Saturday morning. She asked her mom, who said yes, and texted Adelyn back:

"I'm in. Can your parents pick me up at nine?"

Adelyn replied with a thumbs up and a picture of a soccer ball.

The next day, as she waited outside for Adelyn's family to show, Alyssa thought about how STEM class hadn't been as bad as she thought it would be without Adelyn. It seems like Adelyn's soccer was taking A LOT of time. Maybe she wouldn't have even had too much time for STEM if she had done both. Ethan was cool, and she liked Ms. Powers. And the projects were fun.

She was interrupted by a van honking and hands waving at her.

"Alyssa!"

"Hi Adelyn!"

They spent the ride catching up with each other. It was nice to spend time with a friend.

The group arrived at the soccer fields. The place was HUGE. Alyssa figured there must have been fifteen fields. She did some math in her head…..eleven players per team….two teams per game…plus several backup players…lets say two teams of twenty… fifteen fields times forty players, that's six hundred players….maybe two spectators per player….that's twelve hundred more people…. Maybe eighteen hundred people?

She didn't say any of her math out loud, but Alyssa liked to play with numbers in her head sometimes. It was fun.

They walked towards the fields. Alyssa asked Adelyn: "So, what position are you going to be playing today?"

Adelyn replied: "Goalie."

Alyssa asked: "Cool. You must be pretty good at it."

Adelyn replied: "Maybe. We'll see.."

Alyssa asked: "What do you mean?"

Adelyn replied: "Well, when I started the season, I was playing midfield. And it was alright. But I asked the coach after a week if I could play goalie. That's what my older brother plays. That's what I've always wanted to do. And I thought if I could learn to play goalie, he could show me tips and tricks, and we could practice at home together. Coach is going to start me, and we'll see how things go."

Adelyn saw her team. "I better head over. See you after the game!"

Alyssa found a seat on the bleachers and watched the team do their warmups. She looked for Adelyn. She saw her at the goal, staring intently at the center of the field, like a catcher in baseball watching the pitcher. People were practicing shooting against her.

When the starting whistle blew, she heard cheers of parents and siblings. She heard Adelyn's mom yelling... and also a familiar voice. She couldn't place it. But it sounded familiar.

She looked around to see where the voice was coming from, and as she turned, she ran into the face of …. Ms. Powers. Ms. Powers?

Ms. Powers smiled at Alyssa and said: "Hello Alyssa! Nice to see you. I saw you come in, but I didn't want to embarrass you by having your teacher yell out your name in a public place. Some of my students don't care for that." Ms. Powers winked.

Ayssa liked Ms. Powers. "I don't mind. So, what are you doing here? Do you know someone playing?"

Ms. Powers replied: "Indeed. My niece is playing. And who are you here to see?"

Alyssa replied: "Oh I'm here to see my friend Adelyn. She's playing goalie on the far side…the one in the orange shirt." Alyssa pointed at Adelyn.

Ms. Powers said: "Ah, yes. I've seen her around the school. Very good."

Ms. Powers continued: "Well, if you don't mind me asking, how are you liking class?"

Alyssa replied: "I like it. Ethan is a good partner, and you've been helpful when we have questions. It's not quite what I thought it would be, but it's fun."

Ms. Powers asked: "What did you imagine it would be?"

Alyssa responded: "Not sure. Computers?"

Ms. Powers smiled and said: "Yes, it's easy to think it is all about computers."

"STEM is all around you. It's in these benches we are sitting on, it's in how big the soccer field is, it's in the goals, it's in the shoes the players are wearing, even their socks! If you ask the right questions, almost anything can be STEM. You have to look for it. And I've seen plenty of soccer fields."

Alyssa asked: "What do you mean? You've been to a lot of your niece's games?"

Ms. Powers responded: "Well, yes, I've been to several. But I used to play soccer."

Alyssa replied: "Yeah, my dad plays in a city softball league."

Ms. Powers smiled and said: "Yes, I played in a league as well. But I had to travel a bit further for my games."

Alyssa asked: "Your games were out of town?"

Ms. Powers smiled and responded: "Sometimes even out of the country."

Alyssa raised her eyebrows quizzically.

"Many many years ago, I used to play major league soccer. I played for about ten years. It was tough. I remember we had running practice for an hour. And THAT was before the two hour practice started!"

Alyssa's eyes grew wide. Her teacher was apparently full of surprises.

"When I was younger, my body could handle it. But I'm a bit older now, and my body said I should take a break. So I did. I moved here ten years ago. And I decided to hang up my cleats and try out teaching. I decided to try teaching. And I like it. So here I am!"

Alyssa looked at Ms. Powers with astonishment and asked: "So you played soccer against other countries?"

Ms. Powers responded: "Indeed. It was quite a ride."

Alyssa said: "Why didn't you tell us this in class? Everyone would think it is so cool!"

Ms. Powers replied: "Well I don't like to brag about it. But perhaps we can watch one of my games in class before the end of the year."

Alyssa replied: "That would be awesome. I know I would love to see it and other kids would too."

Ms. Powers said: "Speaking of class — your video of you and Ethan was especially good. You did a great job. It got right to the point, was simple, and wasn't too long. I like when students turn in an assignment that's simple and explains the basic concepts well. It shows me they understand it."

Alyssa was surprised Ms. Powers seemed almost happy about it being short.

Alyssa replied: "Yeah, it was short, but hopefully we got all the main points. I kind of got that feeling too when we were explaining our class to the fifth graders." Alyssa pointed down the row to Adelyn's younger sister Sophia and said: "That's actually the fifth grader Ethan and I talked to. She's my friend's younger sister."

She continued: "I'm glad you liked our video. I also sent it to my uncle. My Uncle Mikey works at NASA, and I talk with him about class sometimes. I haven't heard back from him yet on the video though. I hope he likes it."

Ms. Powers asked: "Does it matter?"

Alyssa responded: "I guess so. I mean, he works at NASA after all."

Ms. Powers asked: "Do you think it was good?"

Alyssa replied: "Yeah, I think so. And you said it was good."

Ms. Powers said: "You and Ethan did a fine job. And I'm sure your uncle is extremely good at what he does. It's good to have friends and people who help you. But it's even better to be able to be a good friend to yourself. Sometimes you're on the field alone. But not forever."

The families stood up and cheered. Adelyn made a big save at the goal. Alyssa cheered.

CHAPTER 15

It was time for Alyssa and Ethan's big day. The school Maker Faire was coming up on Saturday.

On Friday afternoon, Alyssa agreed with Ethan that she would bring the Crane Kit from the classroom to her house for final testing, and she would be the one to bring it to the school on the weekend. Alyssa had brought a cardboard box from home to pack the kit in. She cautiously put the fully assembled Crane Kit in the box. She smiled proudly.

On Friday night, after double checking she had everything ready for the next day, she decided to take a break and headed for the kitchen. She heard her brother Lincoln yell: "The animal crane is back! It's back!"

Fearing her little brother was about to destroy her prized creation, she quickly went to her room to check on him.

There was no destruction happening, but Lincoln was holding several of his favorite stuffed animals. A stuffed squirrel, Clifford the Big Red Dog, and a plush turtle. He was raising his hands and making the crane sound.

She picked up the stuffed squirrel and placed it close to the Crane Kit. It still had the tie wrap on the bandana.

She powered it up and took out her phone. She opened the remote control app, and started to steer the crane arm over the squirrel. She lowered the hook down, grabbed the tie wrap on the bandana of the squirrel, and picked it up. The crane made the sound of the motor pulling up the hook.

Lincoln was thrilled. "Flying! He's flying! Can I try? Can I try?"

Alyssa allowed him to press the buttons on the app. With Alyssa's help, he lowered the crane hook and it picked up the animal again. Lincoln laughed hysterically. It didn't take much for him to be excited. Alyssa had to laugh too. It was easy to laugh when others did.

As she continued to entertain her brother, the idea of bringing a few stuffed animals to the Maker Faire came to her. Their plan had been to demonstrate with keychains and bundles of binder clips, but maybe this would be cooler? She started to doubt herself, wondering if the stuffed animals would make her look like a kindergartener. She wavered, but decided on bringing them. The toys were going to school.

She asked her mom if she could borrow a few smaller stuffed animals from Lincoln. With raised eyebrows, her mom agreed. She ran to the garage for a few more tie wraps for the animals and ran back to her room. She took a picture and texted it to Ethan. She said: "Big brain idea! I'm also going to bring stuffed animals we can pick up tomorrow at the Maker Faire! Like an arcade game."

Ethan texted back: "A little bit cheesy, but I like it. Awesome." He included emoji of a mouse and cheese.

She was so excited about her new idea she forgot to finish her movie. She stayed up for another hour testing the crane could pick up the new stuffed animals. It was working perfectly. She packed everything up in the box and prepared for a good night's sleep. She wasn't too anxious about tomorrow.

The next morning, after a quick breakfast, Alyssa's mom helped her pack up the stuffed animals and a Crane Kit in their car. As they drove to the school, Alyssa answered the standard mom question of "Are you excited about today?" with a half-smile. "Yes", she replied. "I am excited. We made something cool."

While they were still driving, she texted Ethan. "Hey! Are you there yet? We'll be there in like five min."

Ethan texted back: "Yeah, I'm here. Look for me on the right side of the gym. The teachers are setting up the monitors with our video explanations..."

Alyssa cringed thinking about how her video would be on display. She wasn't a big fan of watching herself on video.

When Alyssa and her mom arrived, they opened the trunk to get the box with the animals and the Crane Kit. They started to pull it out together. As they did, Alyssa told her mom: "I got it. I don't need help. I can carry it."

As they walked from their car towards the school, she

saw the soccer field. It reminded her of Adelyn. No Adelyn here today. Her field today was a gym full of projects. And her game was about to start.

As she looked away from the field back towards the school, she shifted the weight of the box to her right hip. She moved her hand to lift up the tilting box, and time started to move in slow motion.

The box started to slip. And slip more. It started to slide. It slid down her arms and she tried desperately to keep it from falling. It felt like time stopped.

When time went back to normal, she heard the Crane Kit hit the ground. She looked in horror. Her hands started to sweat.

Her mom bent down to start picking parts up. She tried to comfort her, like parents do: "It's ok honey, I'm sure everything's fine. We'll get it back together."

Alyssa helped put the pieces back in the box. She let out her frustration. "I don't know. I can't believe I did this. The day of the Maker Faire! Really? Now? I can't believe this."

Alyssa's mom continued on with the classic parent phrases of "It's going to be fine, I promise. It'll be ok." Alyssa didn't believe her.

As they moved pieces back into the box, Alyssa inspected each one before she placed it inside. She saw the crane arm, the hook, the string, those all looked fine. The base, the wheels; they looked good. The circuit board, the motor, and ....

The motor. The motor. She looked at the gear attached to the motor. It was the gear. The gear Uncle Mikey had 3D printed for her. It was there. But it was in two pieces.

Alyssa felt like crying. Her mom noticed she had stopped putting parts back in the box. "Mom! It's broken. The gear! The gear is broken and the kit won't work without it! What am I going to do?"

She tried to comfort Alyssa with a hug, but Alyssa was having none of it. Alyssa said to her mom: "This is the part Uncle Mikey printed for me and sent us! I can't believe THIS is the thing that broke! This is not happening!"

Alyssa's mom said: "Ok, calm down, calm down. Let's figure this out."

They were silent. Her mom's head perked up. "Wait. Didn't you say he sent two of them?"

Alyssa froze. Her mom was right. Uncle Mikey had printed two of the gears. She remembered the post-it note he had put with the gears. It said: "Mistakes happen!" She tried to remember where she had put the extra gear. She thought it was still on her desk in her room.

Alyssa looked at the time on her phone. She had twenty five minutes to be set up before the Maker Faire started. "The extra gear is still in the package Uncle Mikey sent.

It's in my room on my desk. Do you think you can get it in time? Please? Please?"

Alyssa's mom looked at her phone: "Yes. I can. I'll run and get it for you."

Alyssa and her mom quickly carried the box the rest of the way towards the school. They saw Ethan, set down the box, and her mom quickly walked back to the car.

Ethan could tell Alyssa was upset. "Hey. What's wrong? Is everything OK?"

Alyssa said nothing. She picked up the broken gear and showed both pieces of it to Ethan, one in each hand.

"I dropped it."

Ethan asked: "You dropped what? The gear? How could that break it?"

"Everything. I dropped everything. The entire box. I can't believe this."

He was silent. He peered into the box and asked "So the gear broke when it dropped? The same one that had broken before? Is everything else OK?"

Alyssa said: "Everything else is fine. But yes. That's the one. The EXACT same gear. Maybe the gear wasn't strong plastic or something."

He looked at the gear. "So what are we going to do? Where did your mom go? To get some glue?"

Alyssa wiped away a tear. "No, not glue. When my uncle made the gear, he printed and sent two of them. The other one is at my house. My mom went home to get it. I'm crossing my fingers she finds it and comes back in time."

Ethan said: "So what are we going to do if she can't find it?"

Alyssa shrugged her shoulders quietly. "I don't know."

Alyssa watched Ethan start to put the kit back together. It looked like everything else was ok. They powered it on and Alyssa opened up the app to try to move the hook up and down. She clicked the up arrow on the app. She heard the motor move. But saw the hook stay in the same place. No gear, no movement. She sighed.

Alyssa figured if her mom couldn't find the gear, the teachers would be nice and say "Oh it's ok, you guys did great!" But Alyssa would know she didn't do great.

The teacher helping with the monitor setup wheeled in a cart beside their table and started the video of the explanation. And it was on repeat. People would want to see their kit lift and move things, and she could explain she was so amazing that she had broken it just an hour before. Awesome. Just awesome.

As she stared at her broken kit, she saw Ms. Powers walk by with a stack of papers. She wanted to tell her what had happened.

Alyssa took a deep breath, and prepared to tap Ms. Powers on the shoulder. But before she was able to, another teacher tapped on her other shoulder. The other teacher pointed across the room, and asked Ms. Powers to follow.

She sighed. No talking to Ms. Powers for now.

Five minutes to go before the Maker Faire started.

Alyssa watched as the other students tested their projects. She saw Madison and Danny testing their solar powered robot car. They watched as the car went on the ground between the lines of tape they had put on the floor. They could even steer it. The track looked like an "eight". Round and round their car went.

Alyssa kept checking the time on her phone, wondering when her mom would be back. She texted her mom: "Did you find it??? Are you coming soon??? 5 minutes!"

She became even more anxious as she saw more groups with their projects. A mini Ferris Wheel. A five foot long bridge made of straws. A chemistry "slime" demonstration. An optical illusion where it seemed like objects disappeared. She wished she and her project could disappear until they fixed it.

Two minutes until start time. She saw her mom walk in. She RAN towards her.

Her mom gave her the package. Alyssa quickly opened it and pulled the gear out of the bag.

Ethan cleared the area so Alyssa could put it on the motor. She took another deep breath, and pushed the gear on, hoping it didn't break. As she pushed with a bit more force, she felt a satisfying "snap". It was on. Perfect fit. She sighed a sigh of relief.

She turned to Ethan.

Ethan nodded his head.

She closed her eyes and held her breath as she pressed the button on the app to raise the hook. Ethan shouted: "It's going up! It's going up!"

They did their final checks. Even their "Rudolph the Red-Nosed Reindeer" tune was playing when she expected it. Alyssa breathed out. Right on time.

Uncle Mikey told her fixing was always easier the second time.

Ethan readied the stuffed animals to be lifted by the hook, and Alyssa situated their kit on the table so the judges and visitors could have a good view.

For the next hour, families, teachers, and judges came up to the booth. A young toddler with a family came by extremely excited about the crane picking up animals. The toddler pulled his parents to the booth and shouted: "Look at it, mom! It's picking it up! Like the game!"

Behind the family, Alyssa saw a teacher with "JUDGE" on the nametag. She saw the judge smile and make a note on his clipboard. It was always nerve-wracking to watch someone else writing notes about you.

She must have watched one hundred families and teachers walk by their booth to see their improvised arcade game. She was sick of hearing herself and Ethan on the monitor next to them. She had almost memorized their entire speech. She'd probably hear it in her head when she went to sleep.

She heard someone tap on a microphone. "Hello, hello? Is this thing on? Ah, there it is, okay."

She saw Ms. Powers in the middle of the gym. Ms. Powers addressed the crowd: "Thank you all for coming. We teachers are all incredibly proud of our students today. They've all completed some pretty amazing projects. Let's give them a round of applause, eh?"

The audience clapped. Alyssa awkwardly clapped, not knowing if she was clapping for herself.

Ms. Powers continued: "The students have been working with their kits for several months now. And although you see the finished product today, I'm sure their path to get here was filled with success and failure. I'm sure there were things that went wrong, and parts that went right."

Alyssa thought she saw Ms. Powers look at her, but she wasn't sure. She figured she was just being paranoid.

Her teacher announced: "And now, the moment I'm sure all the students have been waiting for, the judges' results! Please welcome our lead judge, Miss Armstrong!"

Ms. Armstrong took the microphone from her fellow teacher: "It is my pleasure to announce the winners of today's Maker Faire! The groups were judged on both the quality of their explanations, and their demonstrations and their exhibits."

"For third place, we would like to recognize the ……. Solar Car! Come on up! Come on up!"

The clapping started, followed by Madison and Danny making their way to the front. The group proudly held up their mini electric car and faced the audience as Ms. Armstrong handed them their trophy and parents took pictures.

Alyssa figured they had a chance at either first or second. She had a good feeling. She and Ethan may have even pulled out first place today.   Maybe the animal crane hadn't been too cheesy. She did see a judge laugh. Hopefully it had been a good laugh. She crossed her fingers. She tried to get an idea by watching the judges eyes.

A judge handed another piece of paper to Ms. Armstrong. She pushed up her glasses and announced: "And for second place, we have the stuffed animal crane!". The audience laughed, probably when they heard "stuffed animal crane". Alyssa was a little embarrassed. She wasn't thrilled to have gotten second, but she still put on a halfway-real smile.

Alyssa and Ethan received their medals and trophy while their parents took pictures.   They shook the judges hands, and made their way back to where they had been standing.

She looked up just in time to hear the first place winner being announced. "And for first place, we have the Moving Catapult group!" Alyssa had seen the catapult. They had a target for the beanbags thrown from a robot catapult. She had to admit it was pretty cool.

After the first place group was awarded, the applause died down, and the teachers thanked everyone for coming.

Both Alyssa and Ethan had gotten a medal, but there was only one trophy to share between the two of them. Alyssa looked towards Ethan. She handed the trophy to him. "Pretty cool, right? I wish we had gotten first….. but, I guess considering we almost didn't compete at all, I'm glad we got second."

Ethan smiled as he looked at the trophy. "Yeah, I'm cool with it."

He handed the trophy back. "You should keep it."

Alyssa hesitantly accepted. "Why? Why should I be the one to keep it?"

Ethan replied: "You should have it. You were so excited about this class you took the kit home a few times!"

The group started walking back to pack up. Alyssa's

mom leaned towards her ear. "Alyssa, I know you two didn't get first today, but I've got a consolation prize."

Alyssa figured they were going to go out to eat or have ice cream. She'd be good with that. She already had the place picked out.

Alyssa asked: "Are we going to go somewhere?"

Her mom responded: "Yes."

"Where? To the ice cream place by our house?"

"I suppose we could stop there. But not exactly what I had in mind. How about...I'll let you guess. Let's play twenty questions."

Alyssa rolled her eyes. "Really? Twenty questions? I'm not in first grade anymore."

"Come on", said her mom. "It'll be fun. You'll never guess."

CHAPTER 16

Alyssa sighed. "Alright, I guess I'll play. As long as you promise not to use baby voices with me."

Her mom promised: "No baby voices. Got it. Alright. I'm ready for the first question."

"Is it a thing?" Alyssa asked.

Her mom responded: "Kind of. Yes. It's a thing."

Alyssa shook her head at her first question. Not super helpful.

"Is it going somewhere?'

"Yes. It is going somewhere. WE are going somewhere."

"Is it somewhere we have been before?"

"No."

Alyssa couldn't think of why they would go somewhere she hadn't been before. "Come on, how are we gonna get there? What are we gonna do, fly?"

"Yes."

"What??!!? We are flying somewhere? Where are we going?!?!"

Her mom held up her finger. "Ah-ah, remember, yes or no questions only."

"Okay, okay. Umm. Are we going to see family?"

"Yes."

"Are we going to see Uncle Mikey?"

"Kind of."

"What do you mean kind of? That doesn't make any sense!"

They pulled into the driveway. Her mom put the car in park.

"Alright, alright. I guess we can stop with the questions. Here, I'll let someone else explain."

Alyssas mom pulled out her phone and tapped a few buttons. She started a FaceTime call. Alyssa saw the name "Mikey".

She saw Uncle Mikey's face on the screen. "Hello?"

"Uncle Mikey! My mom called you and said you are going to tell me what's going on. What is happening? I'm so confused!"

Alyssa looked at her mom and back at the phone. "She said we are 'kind of' going to come and visit you? Doesn't make any sense!."

Her uncle laughed. "Haha, yeah. But before I tell you what's going on, congratulations on getting second place! Your mom texted me."

She was happy her uncle seemed proud. "Yeah, we were hoping for first. We had a good idea of having the crane pick up stuffed animals. I thought it might be good enough to get us first, but we got second. Oh well. But we can talk about it later. What is going on here? Are we going to visit you or what?"

Her uncle responded. "Yes."

"In California?"

"No."

She furrowed her eyebrows. "What? Not where you live?"

Uncle Mikey adjusted his hat. "Florida. You are coming to visit me in Florida."

"Why on earth would we go there? That's not where you live."

"No, definitely not. Soo...you remember the launch of the Mars Rover is coming up, right?"

Her mind started racing. Was she seriously going to go to the launch?

"Yes...I remember. Around Thanksgiving, right?"

"Yep. Around Thanksgiving. And your family usually takes a trip around Thanksgiving, right?"

Alyssa responded. "Yeees. So you're telling me. That we. WE? WE are going to Florida at Thanksgiving to see the launch?"

Uncle Mikey smiled. "You got it. Remember your Aunt Megan lives there? We are going to stay with them. And I was able to get tickets for you and I to be able to see the launch up close. With me. It was REALLY hard to get tickets to the launch, and I am only able to bring one person to see it up close. And I chose you!"

Alyssa couldn't speak. After a few seconds, she asked: "Wait. We are going to see the launch. Up close. In person. With you? Are you serious? Really really?"

"Really really. Yes, that's the plan. You and your family will be coming to Florida for Thanksgiving to spend it with me, your Aunt Megan and Uncle Ben, and their family. The rest of the family will be able to see it from the beach."

Alyssa was in shock. She looked at her mom. She looked at her uncle. Then back and forth a few more times.

She wanted to make sure this was real. "Are you serious? This is actually happening?"

Her uncle nodded, as did her mom. Her mom smiled.

They unbuckled their seatbelts and went inside. Alyssa

walked with her mom's phone. "I still can't believe this. This is crazy."

Alyssa stopped. "Wait. Don't you have to be at your work when it launches?"

Her uncle shook his head. "My part will come later. The part of the rover I worked on is tucked away nicely inside, not powered on. Our instrument just has to hang on for the ride. In a month or so, we'll power up our instrument to make sure it's responding. But it takes months to get to Mars. My only job at the launch is to watch."

She HAD to text Ethan after their call ended. He would not believe this!

She finished the call telling her uncle about the Maker Faire and all the drama. It was a LONG story.

Less than two seconds after she ended the call with her uncle, she texted Ethan with the news and went up to her room. It was early November, but she started to pack for the Thanksgiving trip. She set out the suitcase she usually used, and started to put in everything she usually took on trips. She heard her phone buzz. She and Ethan had A LOT to talk about.

After what seemed like forever to Alyssa, Thanksgiving break came.

The weekend before their flight, her dad had stopped

by her room multiple times asking her if everything she needed was packed. She answered him the same way all three times he had asked: "Yes. I'm packed." She had been packed for a month.

On the Monday before Thanksgiving, they made it to the airport, through security, through the gate, and finally, to their seats on the plane. They were headed east this time. Not west to California. East to Florida.

She loved taking off. She looked outside as the plane banked. The cities started to get smaller, and eventually, all she saw was the ocean. She heard the pilot announce they had reached cruising altitude over the Gulf of Mexico.

She spent a while looking outside the window. She LOVED looking at the clouds and the ocean.

The flight had free WiFi, so she watched YouTube videos of previous Mars Rover launches. She loved the final countdown. Something inside of her felt magical when she saw the rocket launch.

Before she knew it, she had watched YouTube videos of ALL the Mars Rover launches, a few videos about SpaceX, and the Mark Rober video about the squirrel obstacle course. She watched the squirrel obstacle video course twice.

The plane soon began to descend. Flight attendants came by to pick up trash. She put in her finished cup of Sprite she had asked for. She saw the man across from her put his finished cup of tomato juice into the bag.

Gross.

Alyssa and her family waited their turn to get off the plane, and they navigated the busy Orlando International Airport. They eventually arrived at the stairs leading them to the baggage claim.

As they reached the bottom of the stairs, she saw him. Her uncle. Dressed in the exact same NASA shirt and surfer shorts he had been in when he picked them up in California.

The family made their way to him. She gave him a big hug, as did the rest of the family. Her mom asked Uncle Mikey: "Don't you have any different shirts?"

He fired back: "Yes. I do. I have twenty sets of this exact same outfit."

Alyssa's mom laughed and shook her head.

Uncle Mikey guided the family towards the parking garage. They loaded up and headed for Uncle Ben and Aunt Megan's house.

They arrived at the house, where Alyssa saw her cousins, some Thanksgiving decorations her aunt had put out, and her uncle talking with his sisters and brother. Alyssa enjoyed her time with her cousins, but she couldn't stop thinking about the launch. It was going to be on the day before Thanksgiving - on Wednesday.

Wednesday finally came. She and her uncle drove to the NASA Kennedy Space Center, where they spent the afternoon at the museum. There were rockets as tall as buildings in the "Rocket Garden". She got close enough to almost touch the Space Shuttle Atlantis, which had BEEN IN SPACE! She saw the Saturn V rocket used for the Apollo moon missions. It was overwhelming. And amazing. And her uncle was her own personal tour guide. Her friends would NOT believe this. She took pictures of everything.

After the museum, she saw Uncle Mikey show his badge to an attendant, and the attendant waved them through. She and her uncle headed towards a bus. He explained to her they were going to take a bus to the launch site, where there would be bleachers they'd be able to view the launch from.

On the way out to the site, the bus driver pointed out the alligators on the sides of the roads. It was a swampy area. She wondered if there were pythons. But she decided she'd rather not think about humongous snakes. She went back to thinking about the launch.

When they arrived at the launch site, she was overwhelmed. She saw men and women in military uniforms, a lot of official looking people with NASA badges on. And there was her uncle. In his NASA shirt and surfer shorts.

Her uncle guided her to the bleachers where they would see the launch from. He pointed at the rocket, and told her the launch would be in about one hour, around dusk.

After they found a seat in the bleachers, her uncle

showed her his phone. "Hey, check this out. This is a livestream of the operations center." She saw official looking NASA polo shirts, people with headsets, and computers. Lots and lots of computers. She thought to herself: "Hackers. Hackers?"

Alyssa's mind snapped back to her visit with Uncle Mikey in California. She remembered everything he had shown her, and what he told her about hacking. Alyssa wondered if she was a hacker now. Maybe a hacker in training?

The time went by slowly. Alyssa was still in shock as she looked around her and back at the rocket, then around her again, then back to the rocket. She FINALLY heard an announcer on a loudspeaker say the launch was in thirty minutes.

Her gaze continued switching back and forth between the countdown clock and the rocket. Twenty-five minutes. Twenty minutes. Fifteen minutes. The last fifteen minutes felt like FOREVER.

Eventually, she saw the clock reach one minute.

The audience became quiet. The loudspeaker started booming at thirty seconds: "thirty..twenty-nine…". Her heart was racing. She pulled out her phone so she could take a video. She HAD to show this to her friends.

She heard the announcer reach ten seconds. She counted along with him. "ten…nine..eight..seven..six..five..four…". Her eyes were locked on the rocket. She saw an orange fire start to form. She could feel rumbling. She saw the tower start to release the rocket.   She heard the announcer: "three..two..one...LIFTOFF!". Her whole body tingled.   Her mind was filled with sparks, just like the engine on the rocket. And just like that, the world's largest LEGO set was on its way to Mars.

THE END

AUTHOR'S NOTE

I wrote this book because I wanted to pass on lessons from twenty years of working in STEM. Complex projects can be frustrating.   But beyond the frustration lies the reward. For me, the joy is in figuring things out. In making things work. I've broken many things, and as a consequence, learned to fix many things.   If you are in the STEM world, trust in your ability to figure out problems. If you find yourself stumped, step back, go easy on yourself, work through the problem, step by step by step. Sometimes you are writing your own LEGO instructions, and you're going to fail a thousand times, but, eventually, you will make it work.

You are now officially a "hacker", at least according to one dad, sitting at a desk, eating chips, trying not to spill a drink on the keyboard, wondering how to write a book.

Scott Miller

http://hackerclassbook.com

hackerclassbook@gmail.com

EDUCATOR'S NOTE

The goal of this book is to use a fun story to teach elementary grade students interested in STEM how to improve their problem solving skills.

The book is meant to encourage the positive traits of the "hacker" culture; focusing on persistence, creativity, self-trust, and a growth mindset. This book aims to teach thinking patterns that help work through the frustration of complex STEM projects, and hopefully come out the other side a bit wiser.

The author graduated from Texas A&M University and has twenty years of experience as a software engineer for NASA missions, military aircraft avionics, and new generations of medical devices. He lives in San Antonio, TX with his wife and three children, a fish, a dog who sometimes listens, and piles of electronics he won't give away.

http://hackerclassbook.com

hackerclassbook@gmail.com

Made in the USA
Coppell, TX
15 February 2022

73626368R00097